"How badly do y[ou want] forty million d[ollars?"]

Penny looked away from Frank Corey's grim face. She didn't want it at all. But she was the only one who knew what her grandfather had wanted done with his money.

"I want that money very much," she said firmly.

"Then you have only ten days to act." Frank sighed deeply. "In that case, Penny, I would like you to marry me."

"I—but—" she spluttered.

"Who else might marry you in such a hurry?" He guided her toward the hotel lounge. "Here I am. We're well acquainted. And you want the money badly, don't you?"

But, she thought, the only thing she really knew about him was that she loved him! And where did that leave her in the face of such a cold-blooded proposal?

EMMA GOLDRICK describes herself as a grandmother first and an author second. She was born and raised in Puerto Rico where she met her husband, a career military man from Massachusetts. His postings took them all over the world, which often led to mishaps—such as the Christmas they arrived in Germany before their furniture. Emma uses the places she's been as backgrounds for her books, but just in case she runs short of settings, this prolific author and her husband are always making new travel plans.

Books by Emma Goldrick

These books may be available at your local bookseller.

Don't miss any of our special offers. Write to us at the following address for information on our newest releases.

Harlequin Reader Service
901 Fuhrmann Blvd., P.O. Box 1397, Buffalo, NY 14240
Canadian address: P.O. Box 603,
Fort Erie, Ont. L2A 5X3

EMMA GOLDRICK

hidden treasures

Harlequin Books

TORONTO • NEW YORK • LONDON
AMSTERDAM • PARIS • SYDNEY • HAMBURG
STOCKHOLM • ATHENS • TOKYO • MILAN

Harlequin Presents first edition February 1987
ISBN 0-373-10953-9

Original hardcover edition published in 1986
by Mills & Boon Limited

CHAPTER ONE

WHEN she turned left, off the paved surface of Route 6A, her mind was on other things. The dirt road bumped and tumbled her 1974 van as she went down the slight incline that lead eventually to the Great Salt Marsh. She did some rapid calculations in her mind. Today had been the last day of the cranberry harvest. She was out of work again. But her savings account was satisfyingly full. There would be no need for further part-time jobs until January. And in January, she would be twenty-one. If she managed to live that long, that is. 'Dear Uncle Henry,' she grinned, 'how I wish you luck—all bad!' There was nothing ever going to destroy her sense of humour, she assured herself. Not even Uncle Henry!

Movement crossed the corner of her eye, and her right foot automatically jammed down the brake-pedal. The brakes were the only part of the old van that worked right, she prayed. Luckily she had been going at less than ten miles an hour, due to the road condition. The back wheels of the van dug into the rock and sand surface of the road with a mighty squeal. Whatever it was that had run out into the road was so close to the front of her van that she could not see it. The truck groaned and squealed again, twisted to the right, slid a little more, and came to a full stop.

She could feel herself shaking. Her hands gripped the steering wheel so hard that she had to pry them free. For one awful moment she berated herself for driving and dreaming. In the confusion the motor had stalled. Wearily she reached for the key and turned off the ignition. A line of perspiration formed on her forehead as the silence closed in on her. The wind whistled in off the beach a quarter of a mile ahead of her, bringing

September's cool kiss. A flock of seagulls swirled over something in the middle of Barnstable harbour, and dead ahead of her she could see the pair of sandpipers who fished the Marsh creeks in defiance of the bigger birds. Nothing else moved.

She opened the driver's door of the van, fumbled with one foot for the step, and backed her lithe five feet ten inches down on to the road. As usual when she was in a hurry, nothing went right. Her foot landed on a rounded pebble, it rolled, and to save herself from falling further, she grabbed at the outside mirror. Her hand slipped on the mirror stanchion and she ended up flat on her well-curved bottom. A pair of sun-warmed blue eyes stared at her. A girl, perhaps nine or ten, no more, dressed in a red gingham dress which was two sizes too small for her, her short blonde hair in wild disarray.

'Hurt yourself?' The little voice was clear and high, and filled with sympathy. The child cuddled a rag doll under her left arm.

'No, I guess not,' Penny sighed. Using the open door for leverage she managed to get to her feet. The flint-like rocks pierced her heavy socks and drew blood. 'Damn!' she muttered.

'You're dressed funny,' the little girl announced. Penny smiled and looked down at herself. A set of men's coveralls, open at the neck to display a red T-shirt. No shoes. Her long, straw-coloured hair tied up in a ponytail with a shoelace. Funny indeed!

'These are my working clothes,' she said very solemnly. 'I wear a pair of rubber overalls and a pair of boots when I'm in the water, but they're all so heavy I take them off when I get through work. In the cranberry bogs. You know about cranberries?'

'Doesn't everybody,' the girl retorted. 'Thanksgiving. They go with the turkey and everything. You almost ran over my ball!' There was just the touch of accusation in the tone. Penny giggled.

'So that's what it was! I was afraid it was—something

alive. What are you doing down here? I'm the only one in the whole wide world who lives on this lane.' She gestured a bit further down the road, to the area where the scrub brush had been cleared away by some hopeful builder. He had bet that the population expansion would reach all the way to Navigation Lane, and had built triplicate houses. The expansion had not come, and now the houses looked as if they might fall down before it did. 'I live in that middle house down there,' she added.

'And we live in the house next door,' the girl giggled. 'We're neighbours. Ain't that something? My daddy said we were way out in the boondocks and wouldn't see nobody for years and years! How about that!'

'How about that,' Penny giggled in return. 'Next door neighbours!' She brushed her not-quite-so-clean hand on the leg of her coveralls and extended it. 'Penny——' and then she stopped. Hiding away for almost a year had taught her many lessons. One of them was that people—even little people—came equipped with tongues. And tongues wagged—all of them. And despite what one might think, eventually the word circulated in places where you wouldn't care to have it known. As, for example, Boston, and Uncle Henry's office in the Harris Foundation. So, even with this cute little devil—'Penny Bloom is my name,' she said. It was perfectly correct. Well, almost perfectly correct. Penelope Bloom Harris she had been christened, twenty years and some odd months ago.

The little hand was swallowed up in hers. 'Abigail Corey,' the child said. 'But you could call me Abby, 'cause we're neighbours. My, your hands are hard. You've got callouses!

'I guess you're right,' Penny chuckled, rubbing the palm of one hand with the other. 'It's hard work, in the bogs.' And after her months as a typist, her weeks behind the counter at a Sears store, and her short try-out in the lawyer's office, she had been more than pleased to find an outdoor job, where a girl didn't have to worry about the boss having octopus arms. Or about the private detectives, nosing around looking for Penelope Harris. The little girl was laughing up at her. Penny put the gloom behind her and smiled back. 'This is a bad place to be playing, Abby,' she continued. 'Why don't you grab your ball and let's go down to my house to play?'

Moments later, after much coaxing, the old van condescended to start. Abby climbed up on to the other front seat and they started down the last hundred yards to home. So far, in the short drive from Route 6A, Navigation Lane had sloped gently downward, through secondary growth and scrub pine. At the clearing where the houses stood the road was a mere four feet higher than the Marshland. Just beyond the houses it plunged down and ran through the middle of the wetlands into the distance, where it eventually came to a dead end near Spring Creek. At low tide, in the driest of autumn seasons, the Marsh stood tufted in stubble, where the salt marsh grass had been cut by enterprising farmers. It left a clear view of the sand dunes on the other side of the bay, where Sandy Neck stood out like a tiny mountain. Penny loved that view, so arranged that the water of the bay itself could not be seen from the house. Some day, she promised herself, I'll explore the whole Marsh. Some day.

The van protested as it went up the slight incline into the parking space in front of her house. Gravel squirted, even though she was driving slowly. She set the hand brake and left the car in gear, just in case. 'Okay, young lady. Home sweet home, next door neighbour. Only you've got to remember, don't play out on the lane. With nuts like me driving, it's dangerous.'

'Oh, you are not,' the child laughed. 'Not dangerous, I mean. You drive fine; not like my daddy.'

And that's something you don't want to get into either, Penny told herself. Every little girl has a mother and father—and I don't want to know anything more about that! I'm sure your mother is beautiful, and your father's good looking. Isn't that the way it goes in the song?

The child turned. 'Look it. The truck didn't come!'

'What truck is that?'

'The furniture truck. We got no furniture. Ain't that something terrible?'

'Well, I guess so,' Penny commiserated. 'Surely you have *something* inside the house?'

'Nope. Two sleeping bags, the camping equipment. Things like that.'

'Oh my!' And I wish I knew something more comforting to say, Penny thought. The poor little kid. Camped out inside a ramshackle house. Look at the child's hair, for goodness' sakes. It looks as if someone put a bowl on her head and cut round the edges. Her dress doesn't fit, her underpants are showing, and I'll bet her shoes are too tight. Look how she keeps fidgeting!

'Our house burned down,' the child offered.

'Oh Lord! Was anyone hurt?'

'Weeeel, not really. Daddy got a little burn on his arm when he came to get me, but he said it wasn't much.'

'And that's why you've moved in here?'

'Daddy said it was the only house available in the whole area. Ain't that strange? I bet there's a million houses on Cape Cod, and this is the only empty one.'

'Only two,' Penny laughed. 'The one on the other side is empty, too. Well, it's been nice, but I have to get inside and get to work. Do come and see me tomorrow?'

'I'd like that,' the child returned. 'Early?'

Penny groaned.

'Oh! Not so early?'

'You've got it, pet. No, climb out the side door. The steps are easier.' She slid out of the driver's seat and opened the double doors in the middle of the van. Abby came along behind her and jumped up, still carrying her rag doll as if it were a piece of firewood. One quick smile between them and Abby was off and running for home.

'Might as well unload,' Penny mused as she shifted from one foot to the other. Her old worn sneakers were stuck in the back of the door. She pulled off her heavy socks and put on the shoes. The socks, following old habits, were tucked into her boots. For next season? she asked herself. Or is this the last time for me? Where will I be twelve months from now? *Will* I be twelve months from now? A shudder ran up and down her spine. She pulled the boots, her rubber overalls and her two towels out of the van, stuffing them into an old duffel bag she had bought at an Army Surplus Sales store. The sum total of my life, she sighed, as she hefted the loaded bag. The day's physical work had finally caught up with her. She slammed the double doors shut, and started for the front door, towing the heavy bag behind her.

'Hey, you!' The sound came from behind her, in a deep disgruntled male voice. Something out of Tolkien, she told herself. I don't want to look—it might have teeth. 'Hey, you!' Closer this time. Too darned close. A hand fell on her shoulder. She squirmed away from it and turned angrily, both hands up in the classic karate style.

'Keep your hands off me,' she grated. 'And your tongue, too. My name is not *Hey you!*' He was a big man, but perhaps only two or three inches taller than she. In heels she could look him straight in the eye. Right where I'll put my fist, she told herself. His eyes glared at her. Dark, dark eyes that glared into her green ones. A well-shaped man, except for his face. Craggy, deeply lined. It looks like a cliff that somebody's been mining, she thought to herself. And nobody's struck gold there yet! To be honest, at a second look it was not exactly ugly, but then it was a long way from being good-looking, either. Everything was in its proper place, but it just seemed to—to lean to one side! Maybe if I get angry enough, she thought, I might just straighten it all out for him!

'I don't allow my daughter to go riding around with

strangers,' he snarled. 'If it ever happens again, something will be done about it!'

'But you don't mind her playing ball in the middle of the lane, do you?' she snapped back at him. 'That road is so narrow that all the curves are blind. If I hadn't been going slowly I would have hit *her* instead of her ball! What kind of a parent are you—you——' She had been about to say something on the order of 'ugly monster', but for almost the first time in her life she managed to put a restraint on her tongue. Impossible man! What ever happened to all the *Good Guys* in the world? Or is this the only sort of man I can attract? This one and Uncle Henry and Cousin Oscar? Boy, that's a trio to be proud of!

Her hands were still in the basic defensive position, but her fingers were trembling, shaking themselves half to death only inches from his nose. One chop, that's what I'll give him. One chop, and see if that doesn't rearrange his lovely face!

Somehow a message got through to him. He backed away, leaving her with the feeling that he was laughing at her. In fact the right corner of his mouth kept twitching, as if he were having trouble controlling the muscles.

'You're going in the right direction,' she barked at him. 'My property line ends on the far side of the driveway. Keep going. And do me a big favour, take a few *nice* lessons from your daughter. She knows how.' She picked up the rope on her duffel bag and dragged it into the house behind her. As she shut the front door she looked through its little glass insert. He was still standing there, both hands on his hips, and there was no doubt about it, he was laughing. She kicked her duffel bag into the corner behind the hat rack and stormed into the other end of the house, her kitchen. 'Smart guy,' she muttered as she pounded the counter with both fists. 'Smart guy!' The old pendulum clock on the wall struck a feeble six o'clock, and the tiredness of the day came over her again.

Supper. No matter how crazy she felt, she had to
have supper. A girl her size and shape needed to refill
her boiler regularly, or lose all her steam. And that's
something else I've got to do, she told herself. I've been
on hamburger for a week, what with the rush to clear
the 'black' cranberries from the last of the bogs.
Working overtime every day there had just not been
time to stop for shopping, or cleaning—or—Lord, what
I need is a wife to look after me, she sighed as she
reached into the refrigerator freezer and took out the
last two-pound package of hamburger. Leaving it to
warm on the counter, she stumbled upstairs, stripping
as she went, and quickly filled the bathtub. The instant
hot-water heater worked well enough, but the water
itself came from a brackish well. She sighed as tiny
mixtures of red and brown stirred together in the bath.
Dousing it all with bubble bath was the only solution.
What you can't see won't hurt you. Or rather, to be
logical about it, the water may be discoloured, but it's
been boiled, so it's sanitary discoloration, isn't it?

Whatever the colour, her muscles groaned, and she
meant to soak. She slid into the bathtub gingerly, and
tried to stretch out, without success. It was built for
midgets. She turned the hot water on again, and relaxed
until she was almost parboiled, and then shut it off
again. Her shoulder muscles bothered her the most.
Because the season was getting late for 'blacks' they had
been wet-picking. Flooding the bogs, agitating the
water with floating sweepers until the ripe berries broke
free from their trailing vines and floated to the surface.
Then she and two others, equipped with long rakes, had
the job of sweeping the floating berries into the
protecting lee of a floating wooden boom, where a
couple of other workers filled the boxes and sent them
up the conveyor belt to the truck. And everything had
to be done without breaking the skins of the berries!

All day long, eight and sometimes twelve hours a
day. There was nothing particularly strenuous to it,
each movement of the rakes and brooms, but repeated

time after gentle time it left one with sore arms and shoulder muscles. She sank down into the warmth of the water and thanked God for all His blessings big and small.

Besides, she told herself defensively, she was a big girl, and she liked working outdoors. Maybe I should go over to Ocean Spray, the packing co-operative, she thought—or—maybe I'll just sit at home and knit, or walk on the beach. What do they call that? Beachcomber? If Uncle Henry is really looking for me, he'd never think that of his meek and mild niece.

The water was getting cooler. She pulled the shoelace out of her ponytail and shampooed her hair. Which made it seven o'clock when she came downstairs dressed in her heaviest old bathrobe and wearing her shabbiest slippers. She opened the kitchen door to air the house while she glared at the hamburger. What can you do with two pounds of hamburger? A little ingenuity is required, she threatened herself. Plain hamburger was too, too much. Four days this week already, and she was sick to death of it.

'Patties and mashed potatoes?' she mused aloud. 'Meatloaf? Spaghetti?'

'Oh, that would be nice.' A little voice, coming out of the twilight on the back stoop. Penny smiled to herself and went over to the screen door. Bugs were dive-bombing the wire mesh, attracted by the bright kitchen lights.

'Abby? What are you doing out there, child? You should be ready for bed by now, pumpkin.' She opened the door slightly, and the little girl slipped in.

'I'm afraid we don't have a bed,' the child sighed. 'The furniture men didn't come. And we don't got——'

'Don't have,' Penny corrected.

'Yeah—we don't have any pots and pans, and no nothin'. Daddy made us peanut butter sandwiches, but we don't got—don't have any jelly, either, and I'm—I'm hungry!'

'I see.' Penny searched the thin little face. Blue eyes,

amputated blonde hair, creamy complexion, and thin as
a rail. Just what I would like for my—what in the
foolish world are you thinking, Penelope Harris! She
shook her head to clear her mind. Muzzy thinking,
that's what fills the world with wars and famine, she
told herself sternly. But there the little girl was, hands
clasped behind her back, staring up at Penny as if she
knew that Christmas and the Good Fairy had arrived
all at once.

'What is it you like best?'

'Spaghetti. I'm half Italian, you know.'

'Is that a fact? Well, if I make spaghetti, would you
share a plate with me?'

'I think I'd love that better than anything. Can I
help?'

'Why not?' Penny laughed. 'It all comes out of cans
and bottles these days.'

'Didn't your mommy ever teach you to make it from
scratch?'

'No, love.' She ruffled the girl's hair as she started to
gather the ingredients. 'I never had a mommy, dear. She
died when I was born.'

'Why, that's terrible,' Abby declared. 'That's really
terrible!'

'Not really, Abby. It was a long time ago, before I
knew anything at all. I don't even have a picture to
remember her by. Now, as soon as I get this water
boiling we'll pitch in the spaghetti, and then—this
bottle of sauce has all the ingredients we need. Look on
the bottom shelf of the refrigerator, Abby, and see if
I've got any of that Mozzarella cheese. Yes, that's the
package. And the water's boiling, so in twelve minutes
the spaghetti will be ready, and we can eat. If I can find
the plates. How about that! I've got four plates, and I
can't find—oh, here they are. Want to set the table?'

It was a case where two extra hands made four times
more trouble, but Penny laughed through it all. There
was something tugging at her heart, something she
could not define or refine. The child chattered twenty

miles to the minute, and needed only a little prompting
to move from any one subject to another. That's it,
Penny finally concluded. I missed it all. I wish I could
have had a mother to grow up with. Grandfather was a
stern old Puritan, who prayed every day that I might
have been a boy. Abby's family has given her a million
loving remembrances; all Grandfather ever gave me
was money.

'So tell me about the fire at your house,' she
prompted.

'Oh my, was that ever something. We were all asleep.
Daddy sleeps downstairs—well, he did when we had a
downstairs, and I slept upstairs. And then there was
something wrong with the heater thing—the boiler?'

'Yes, boiler. We don't have one in this house. Go
ahead.'

'Well, it blowed up, like a Star Wars or something,
and Daddy got out of the house, and—but I couldn't
get down the stairs 'cause they were burning, you know.
Daddy came back in the house and got me, and the
firemen all arrived, and it was exciting, but I was too
scared to enjoy it, and they put up a ladder, and Daddy
carried me down. But the house got all burned down!'

'And just when was all this?'

'The day before yesterday. We spent the night at an
Inn but Daddy wanted a real house, and——'

'Where's your mother?'

Two little tears formed in the corners of those blue
eyes. 'I don't have a mother, either. She went off with
somebody else, and she and Daddy, they got a—a
divorce.'

Oh me, Penny thought. What a trap this could be. A
little girl who needs a mother, and she's looking me
over as a suitable candidate. Just the way *I* used to do.
But I never found one, did I, and yet I managed to
survive.

Yeah, sure you did, her conscience snapped at her.
You survived, if that's what you call what you're doing.
All bound up in your grandfather's ethics, running from

your uncle—yeah, you survived. Just barely. Give this girl a little love, you can spare it. But keep your distance from that monster of a father of hers! Him you could do without!

'I—Abby.' Penny dropped down on to one of the rickety kitchen chairs and held out her arms. The little girl ran across the kitchen and threw herself into them. The tiny blonde head nestled just under Penny's chin. She consoled without words. She didn't know any words that fitted. What does a mother say to a stricken daughter? I haven't the slightest idea! What would Grandfather have said? 'Harrises don't cry. You have to be tough to survive.' Sure you do. That's what I am—tough. And who wants a tough woman? Her arms squeezed just the tiniest bit more. The child wiped her eyes on the lapels of Penny's robe.

'I think the spaghetti is boiling over,' she said, in that soft high voice that was so attractive.

The noodles had cooked just long enough. Penny drained them, leaving them in a colander on the stove, over a pan of hot water. 'Supper is served,' she announced. 'Right after you wash your hands, young lady.'

They sat at table quietly for a moment, and to Penny's surprise the little girl piped up with a short but lovely grace. And then they dug in.

'You certainly know how to handle spaghetti,' Penny noted in some awe a minute later. The child, using fork and spoon was doing twice as well as her adult companion. 'I usually cut mine up with a knife,' Penny confessed.

'Huh!' the child returned. 'That's kid stuff. Look, here's how to do it. Didn't you put cheese on it?'

'No, I guess I didn't, Abby. I'm afraid I'm a little tired tonight. I——'

A thunder at the back door interrupted. The screen door squeaked open, and then shut again with a crash. 'Just what the hell is going on here?' he demanded.

Penny looked up at him, startled. He seemed to have

that effect on her. Their second meeting, in *her* house, and she was still jumping out of her skin. Heavy eyebrows, she noted as he stepped into the brilliant light. Look at him glaring at me! You'd think he was about to club me for kidnapping his daughter. And that was when her blood steamed.

'It's called feeding,' she snarled at him. 'That's what I'm doing, feeding your daughter. Peanut butter sandwiches! Yuck!'

'They're very nutritional,' he glowered. 'Who gave you permission to feed my daughter?'

'I didn't need permission,' she snapped back. 'When someone is hungry, you don't have to fill out a questionnaire first! What kind of a father are you, anyway?'

'I'm the kind who doesn't take kindly to people enticing my daughter into affairs——'

'Affairs?' Penny threw down her napkin and stood up. 'Why you——'

'There are plenty of places you could have picked to live,' he snarled at her. 'Why here? Because of us?'

'Why you ... you ...' she stuttered in rage. Cool down, she yelled at herself. Cool down. She took a deep breath. 'For your information, Mr Corey,' she said in her husky contralto voice, 'I've been living in this house for the past six months. Now perhaps you would care to tell me why you violated my privacy by moving in next door?'

'Six months?' There was a doubtful expression on his face as he looked her up and down. For the first time she became aware of the way she was dressed—or undressed. The old robe had fitted her well when she was sixteen. At twenty, it wasn't doing as well, not by a long shot. Nervously her fingers plucked at the lapels, then shifted to the belt and re-tied the knot. There was no way she could properly rearrange it. Although at sixteen she had been a shapely schoolgirl, at twenty she had added several crucial inches at top and bottom, and all of it showed!

'That looks like a lovely meal,' he said. The change of tone and subject threw her off track. He was looking at her, not at the food. How could such an—ugly—man have such a charming daughter, she asked herself, and then quickly decided that she didn't want to know. There was something about him—some aura, some intangible feeling of strength and command—and I don't want to know!

'I'll bet Daddy's hungry too,' Abby piped up. 'She makes wonderful spaghetti, Daddy. Just like Italian. And her name is Penny, and she don't have a mother either. I forgot to ask, Penny, don't you have a daddy, either?'

Penny tried to swallow on a dry throat, tried to break eye contact with him, and failed at both. 'I—no,' she sighed, 'I don't got a—I haven't a father either. He died in the war, before I was born.' She looked from one to the other of them. Two matched pairs of eyes were watching her. 'If you're hungry, Mr Corey?'

'Well, I wouldn't say no to a real Italian dinner,' he laughed. The left corner of his mouth split open in a one-sided grin as he stepped closer to her and put out a hand. 'Frank,' he said. 'Frank Corey, lawyer.'

She fumbled one of her hands out of the pockets of her robe where she had been valiantly trying to stretch the material. 'Penelope—er—Bloom,' she returned. 'Beachcomber. Please have a chair.' She tried to pull her hand back. He parted with it reluctantly, and sat down beside his daughter. Penny rushed to the cupboard over the sink and selected the least cracked of her two remaining plates. The fumbling for the plate, and extra cutlery, gave her time to gather her wits about her. Do I stay here and eat with him, dressed as I am, she asked herself, or do I make some fool excuse to run upstairs and at least put on something that covers me? She could not quite decide, and left it alone. He nodded thanks as she put the plate down in front of him.

'Help yourself,' she said, and remembered that only the sauce was on the table. She scooped up his plate again, went back to the stove, and piled it with noodles. He piled on the sauce and took a tentative sampling.

'Say, that's good,' he remarked. She stalked back to her own place and settled down again. 'You're some kind of cook,' he continued. 'You're Italian, of course?'

'No,' she snapped, and refused to make another comment about it. Her limited cooking experience had all been garnered the hard way, by trial and error. He dipped into the food.

'Beachcomber?' he asked.

'It's an honourable profession,' she said. 'It rates somewhat higher than lawyers and used-car salesmen. Although up until five o'clock today I was a sweeper in a cranberry bog.' And what do you make of that, kind sir?

'That's a pretty muscular trade,' he commented between bites.

'I'm a pretty big girl,' she returned.

'Why, so you are,' he said, with a touch of surprise in his voice. Somehow or other Penny could not quite decide whether he was commenting on the 'pretty' part of her statement, or the 'big'. It left her with a—nice—feeling. Maybe he's not as ugly as I thought, she found herself musing.

Her erratic kitchen clock was striking nine before they were finished. 'I wish I could have offered wine,' she said as she got up to clear the table. 'Would you like some coffee? I'm afraid I don't have a great deal of milk. They don't deliver this far out.' Much to her surprise he had risen at the same moment she had, and as she picked up the sauce boat his hand came down on top of hers. Her squeak was a genuine note of terror. The last thing in the world she needed right now was some physical involvement with a man—any man. Her squeak brought a smile.

Abby tried to help. With one small sink, three plates, and a couple of pots there was too much help for the working area. Standing at the sink, trying to work but keeping out of the traffic zone, Penny suddenly found

him hard up against her as he tried to dodge his
daughter, who was struggling with the last of the
water glasses. He turned round, still pressed close
against her.

'Say, I'm sorry about that,' he chuckled. Both his
hands were on her shoulders. To steady her? She was
backed up against the sink itself, and was in no danger
of falling. But her dignity was upset.

'I wish you wouldn't do that,' she said coldly, looking
down to where his hands seemed to be burning through
her robe. There was a moment of absolute silence.

'Yes, of course,' he said, and moved his hands away.
But again there was something in his voice. Some—
regret? Come off it, Penny! Regret? The man's a
monster. How in the world could he possibly have sired
this beautifully yawning daughter? Yawning?

'Look at that,' she said softly. 'The poor kid is dead
to the world, and I suppose she has school tomorrow?'

'Not exactly,' he returned. And now she received the
full force of those predatory eyes. 'She doesn't go to
school right at this moment. But I'm sure she's tired.
We've been sleeping around lately, and she doesn't rest
well in strange beds.'

'Oh, your furniture didn't arrive?'

'No,' he remarked sadly, 'it looks like another
camping night for us. Bedrolls on the floor.'

'But she can't——' Penny snapped her mouth closed
with a mighty effort, before the rest of it got out. She
can't sleep on the floor, the poor kid. And I've got a
spare bedroom, as well as twin beds in my own room.
But if I finish the sentence, how much trouble am I
inviting? Let the daughter stay while I chase her father
back to his sleeping bag? Ignore them both and hope
they'll go away? What to do? They were both staring at
her, Abby with her blue eyes wide open, her face
hopefully optimistic. He with that one-sided grin that
changed his face and made him seem almost—not ugly.
What was that Arab fable about the camel getting his
nose into the tent? And then came the final straw. A

patter of rain on the back stoop, beginning as a little trickle, then assuming monsoon proportions.

She sighed. 'You can't take Abby back to a bedroll in this rain. I have a spare bedroom. Why don't you—you both spend the night?'

'It won't be too much bother?' he asked politely. She snapped around to stare at him. Those black, black eyebrows, over dark blue eyes. Neanderthal, that face! A primitive man. And the sparkle behind the eyes, the twitch at the corner of his solemn straight mouth. Why, damn it, he's laughing at me again, she raged to herself. Damn the man!

'Not at all,' she answered primly. 'Come on, Abby, let's get you a bath and tuck you in.' The child extended a trusting hand and went with her, leaving her father beside the sink full of dirty dishes.

For once the bathwater ran clean. Penny improvised a nightgown from one of her lightweight shirts, and the child was soon tucked up in one of the twin beds in her own room. 'Can you tell me a story?'

Another crisis, Penny told herself. But it's good training for when—if ever—you get to be somebody's mother, isn't it? Her busy mind spun a turn or two, and threw out a modified version of the 'Three Bears'. The child giggled for the first few minutes, and then was silent. Penny pulled herself out of her own little dream world and took a good look. Abby was fast asleep.

Dishes! Before she went down to do them, Penny slipped into a floor-to-neck flannel nightgown, then donned her robe and crept downstairs. He was in the kitchen washing the last of the pots, and humming a tune. He whirled around when she made a noise behind him.

'You didn't have to do that,' she said.

'You didn't have to feed us,' he returned. That lopsided grin was back again.

'I don't understand why a lawyer would want to live in a dump like this,' she sighed.

'You've been here long enough,' he returned. 'Surely

you know that Cape Cod is no longer just a summer playground? People are flocking into these towns as if it were another Gold lode. There isn't anything in the way of housing.'

'But you could have gone to a motel, or something.'

He dried his hands carefully on the dish towel and came over to her. Both those hands were on her shoulders again, and even the addition of a nightgown under the robe could not reduce the heat and strength of them.

'Our house didn't burn down by accident,' he told her. 'And that's why Abby isn't going to school right now. We need to be out of the way—somewhere that people wouldn't expect us to be. You *do* understand?'

Yes, she told herself, that's something I can understand. That's exactly why *I'm* here. So that some particular people won't think to look—and—but why? Why does he have to be worried about people finding him? He says he's a lawyer. He looks more like a—a mobster. Could that be? That he's some sort of gangster in hiding, or something? No wonder his wife ran off with somebody else.

But having settled on that little bit of mental knitting, he immediately set about unravelling the whole thing. He pulled her closer, the shadow of his head blocking out the overhead light, and his lips touched hers, gently, softly, warmly, and all of Penny Harris's vaunted coolness and control bustled down the kitchen sink along with the swirling water.

CHAPTER TWO

SHE was sure she would never get to sleep. Her bedroom was small, hardly big enough to hold the twin beds and a bureau, and the roof sloped down around a dormer window. The rain continued all night—dripping, drizzling, at times slashing at the house. The weather matched her state of mind. Am I really such a fool? she asked herself over and over again. Here I am, sharing my house with a man whom I hardly know. He *may* be a lawyer, but I wouldn't bet on it. Gangster, probably. Would Uncle Henry have hired a man like that to track me down? She shivered, and tried to push the thought away. It would not go. Uncle Henry would do anything, she was firmly convinced. And if hiring a—man—like this one was all he could do, then yes, he would do it! The Philip Harris Foundation held forty million dollars in trust under Uncle Henry's control, and that's not exactly chicken-feed, is it?

The little girl was snoring softly. Penny found herself counting the rhythm. Her eyes closed, and suddenly it was morning. The sun was high, the raucous raid of seagulls was in full spate, and the little girl was gone. She checked her alarm clock, rattling it in disgust. It was set, as usual, for six o'clock, but had run itself down. Feeling more than a little embarrassed, she grappled for her robe, swished her feet around on the cold linoleum, and finally found her slippers. A hostess certainly ought to be up and prepared to feed her guests, she told herself. There was no noise from the spare room, but she hesitated to open the door. Only the Lord knew what she might find there. 'And I don't want to know,' she said under her breath as she started for the stairs.

'I don't want to know!' That's getting to be my

23

favourite phrase, isn't it, Penny—er—Bloom! She brushed the hair out of her eyes and shuffled, bleary-eyed, into the kitchen. Empty! So they've gone out and about already? I'll get them some breakfast and wish them happy on their way, that's what I'll do, she determined. One of her eyes was determined not to co-operate. She fumbled her way to the sink and splashed water on the culprit. Her aim was bad. The cold water ran down her face, her neck, to course down between her breasts and over her stomach. She shivered, and managed to pry the offending eye open. Things seemed clearer in stereo. She started the water heating for instant coffee, and stalked over to the refrigerator. And there was his note, hanging on the refrigerator door.

'Have to go to work,' it said in a bold blunt writing style. 'Look after Abby. Buy her some clothes.' Under the magnet that held the note to the metal door was a twenty-dollar bill. She plucked it out, fell back into the nearest chair, and bellowed for all she was worth. Buy the child some clothes with twenty dollars? Good lord, no wonder Abby is half naked. This—man—hasn't any idea what it costs these days! If they were lucky, twenty dollars might buy a pair of shoes, perhaps. Prices ran high on the Cape, as on any summer resort area—even after the summer had gone.

The kettle whistled at her. She slammed the bill under the sugar bowl and went to make herself some coffee. She crouched over the steaming mug, like a witch over her cauldron. 'And looking it, too,' she reminded herself as she caught a glimpse in the tiny mirror over the sink. Hair all awry, a disreputable bathrobe, a nightgown that had seen more than one better year! Maybe I'm lucky that he's gone. To work? All the banks opened at nine, and the clock said ten. Good time for a bank stick-up? Or maybe he specialises in kidnapping, or something! Lawyer? Huh! What a nerve he's got. Without even a by-your-leave he dumps his daughter on me and goes off 'on his job'. What an arrogant, homely——

Her diatribe was interrupted by a truck horn, one of

those diesel truck trumpets, that sounded like the Archangel's last peal. It snapped her up out of her chair, making her spill half her coffee down the front of her robe. A moment later there was a thunder at her front door. 'Oh lord,' she muttered, 'look at me.' The pounding grew heavier. She stopped by the stairs, Perhaps there was time to slip upstairs and at least put on a pair of slacks? The house shook with the thundering. One more assault, she sighed to herself, and it'll collapse into a pile of sticks.

'I'm coming!' she yelled. 'I'm coming!' Clutching the lapels of her robe in one hand, she slippered across to the front door, struggled with the baulky lock, and opened it just a hair. A huge moving truck stood in front of the other house. 'Turner Brothers', the sign on its side said. And here in front of her were two of the bulkiest men she had ever seen. Obviously, the Turner brothers? She opened the door another inch or two. 'Well?' she challenged.

'Furniture,' the one closest to her grunted.

'How nice,' she offered. 'I don't want any.'

'For next door,' the other man told her. 'He left this note on the door.' He handed her a crumpled piece of paper. 'See lady next door,' it said.

'Well, you've seen all of me you're going to,' she said stubbornly. 'Now will you please go away!'

'You have to tell us where you want the furniture, lady.' She scanned their faces. No doubt about it, they were prepared to be as stubborn as she.

'Dump it in the driveway,' she suggested hopefully.

'We don't do that kind of service, C'mon, lady. It won't take you any time at all, and we got four more deliveries to make this morning. Our time's valuable.'

She was just about to retort that *her* time was valuable too, when she suddenly remembered that it wasn't. Not the least. Her job was finished. As a lady of leisure she was entitled to lay around all morning if it suited her. Lady? Hah! 'I have to get dressed,' she muttered. 'Ten minutes.'

'We ain't got ten minutes to spare,' the brothers Turner informed her.

'The hell you haven't,' she replied grimly as she slammed the door in their faces and ran for the stairs. She lost one slipper half-way up, and almost did a backward flip all the way back down. Almost! There was no time for selecting. The Turners were hammering on her door again. Briefs. She loved silky lacy briefs, but had to settle for cotton. Dark brown slacks. They fitted loosely. She had lost a deal of weight since she left Boston. After she had left Uncle Henry's employ as a computer programmer and taken up manual labour. One white silk blouse. Exercise had done something for her there, too. The buttons strained to contain her proud breasts, leaving nothing to the imagination. She shrugged her shoulders and reached for her yellow plastic windbreaker, and tied on her flat-heeled brown Tom McAnns. And hurried down the stairs before the door fell off its hinges. She grabbed at the knob and moved it just far enough to evade the next attack.

'Leave my door alone,' she grumbled. I need two cups of coffee, she told herself. How can I possibly live without two cups of coffee? Nobody in her right mind starts the day without some caffeine in her bloodstream! She was still grumbling as she ploughed her way across the drive that separated the two houses. Abby was sitting on the slab of cement that masqueraded as a front step.

'I got the key,' the little girl said anxiously. 'I didn't know what to tell them about anything.' She looked so concerned that Penny's grouch melted. She held out her two hands, taking the child in one, and the key in the other. Behind her the rear doors of the truck slammed open. She looked over her shoulder. The Turner brothers were already man-handling a sofa up the drive.

For an hour she stood in the front door, giving haphazard directions as each piece was brought in. 'You sure you got it right?' Abby pressed.

'If I don't, your—father—can worry about it,' she

snapped, and then relaxed again. 'I'm an awful grouch in the morning.'

'I could get used to that,' Abby returned. 'That's the last of it, I think.'

'Sign here.' The moving man held out a clipboard with multiple copies of a form on it.

'Why?' she demanded.

'I gotta have a signature,' he grunted.

'Or you'll take it all back?'

'Sign the paper, lady!' Another one of them, Penny told herself fiercely. Okay, buddy, if that's the way you feel about it, try this. With a graceful hand she wrote at the bottom of the slip, 'Eleanor Roosevelt'. He scanned it quickly.

'Okay, Mrs Roosevelt,' he grunted.

'Miss,' she corrected him. After all, if you intend to play a game, shouldn't you play it all the way through? The Turner brother tipped a finger to his forehead. 'Can I get back to the main road by going straight ahead?' he asked.

'Sure,' she replied, 'If your truck can float. The road just fades away into the marshes.'

'I used to know an Eleanor Roosevelt someplace,' he muttered, and left.

'C'mon,' Abby said, pulling at Penny's hand. 'You need a cup of coffee.'

'Three,' Penny confessed.

'Boy, you're worse than my dad, and he's a caffeine freak. Mrs Roosevelt. What a fib you told that man!'

'It's what he wanted to hear,' Penny chuckled. 'And don't you talk to me like that. I'm old enough to be your mother.'

'Yeah!' The little girl led her up the front step of her own house. 'Wouldn't that be wonderful!'

Don't say another word, Penny told herself. You put both feet in your mouth at the same time, didn't you! You knew yesterday that the little thing was looking for a mother. What are you, some kind of a nut? The last thing in the world you need is to be somebody's mother. No, that's not right, she corrected herself honestly. Being the kid's mother wouldn't be hard—but you'd have to take the father along with her. Now that's what you could call the height of stupidity, getting emotionally involved with that ugly, ugly man!

But he didn't look all that ugly yesterday when he kissed you, her stubborn conscience insisted. 'Shut up!' Penny snapped.

'What?' Abby asked.

'Nothing. I was talking to myself. Come into the kitchen and let's get some brunch.'

A quick survey of the cupboards indicated that she was in the same state as Old Mother Hubbard. So she made a clean sweep, feeding Abby the last egg, the two tiny slices of ham, a piece of toast, and orange juice. She made do for herself on three cups of coffee, and one half-burnt slice of toast. The child gobbled away as if she hadn't eaten in a week. It's not that she's showing poor table manners, Penny mused, she's just hungry! I wonder if he goes off and leaves her like this all the time? What do they call them? Latchkey children, living out their lonely lives with the front door key strung on a chain around their necks. Poor kid!

'Well, the first thing we've got to do,' she started to say, and then stopped. She had just taken a good look at herself in the mirror, and had done a quick survey of Abby.

'The first thing what?'

'The first thing we're going to do,' she chuckled, 'is to get our hair washed. Both of us!' The job took some time, but eventually, around one o'clock, Penny was sitting on a kitchen chair with Abby standing between her legs as the hair brush smoothed down the child's beautiful hair. 'Was your hair always this short?'

'No. It was long, but it got burned in the fire,' the girl sighed. 'It's a funny thing to fight about, ain't it?'

'Isn't,' Penny said. 'Isn't what?' She was brushing the silky hair, trying to make some order out of it.

'My hair. Mama wanted me to have long hair, and

Daddy said it ought to be short, and they had a terrible fight.'

'Just about your hair?'

'No—not just. But that was the last one. They fought about everything. I don't think they liked each other very much.'

'Don't say that' The heavy deep voice came from the back door as he stomped in, empty-handed. His face was twisted with some emotion Penny could not judge. 'Your mother was a victim of the war,' he said harshly, 'and I didn't have the sense to know it. I should have known. We mustn't blame her for anything. You understand me, Abby?'

The little girl ran to him and was enveloped in his arms as he claimed the only empty chair. Almost automatically Penny reached for the coffee-pot and filled a mug for him. He gave her one quick look of appreciation, and returned to his daughter.

'I—all right, Daddy. I don't really understand, but——' He pulled her closer still, lifting her off her feet and treasuring her tiny face next to his. 'We neither of us must ever blame your mother, child,' he repeated as he rocked her back and forth for a moment, and then turned her loose. He grabbed at the coffee mug desperately, nursed it between his big palms, and then took a sip. The sense of tension left the room. He managed one of those crooked smiles for Penny.

'And what have you been up to?'

'Not much. Your furniture came. We had breakfast. We washed our hair. And I was just about to go food-shopping with Abby.'

'Where? Very far from here?'

'No, not far. I usually go down to the Capetown Mall, to the Heartland Food Warehouse.'

'That's over near Hyannis?'

'Yes. Right across the street from the Cape Cod Mall.'

'Not today.' His grin had disappeared, replaced by a furrow on his brow that emphasised the heaviness of his eyebrows, the coldness that reflected from those dark blue eyes.

'But I have to eat,' she protested. He shrugged his shoulders in a Gallic response.

'We all have to,' he said, 'but Abby can't go. Isn't there some small shop in Sandwich, or someplace like that, where you could pick up enough food to last until tomorrow?'

'I'm sure there is, and I could,' she told him. 'But not without an explanation.' He glared at her, struggling with an answer he didn't want to give. Look at that, she told herself. He's a real problem-child, that one. That's what happens when you let a lawyer move into the neighbourhood—if he is a lawyer. The whole damn area just goes to hell in a handbasket! She mustered up her own glare. There was one stalk of celery left in the refrigerator's cold compartment. She pulled it out, sat down at the table, and began munching on it noisily.

'I suppose you're telling me that's all you've got to eat?'

She shook the remainder of the stalk under his nose. 'That's it,' she returned. 'Today's my grocery shopping day—for me. With a proper explanation, maybe I could shop for you too.'

'Are all women so damn' much trouble?' he muttered.

'Probably,' she snapped back. 'We get that way by associating with men like you. Well?'

'Where's your telephone?' he asked. She shrugged her shoulders.

'I do casual day labour. For that you don't need a telephone. Or can afford one, come to think of it. And telephones are——' Stop right there, her mind screamed at her. Stop right there. This man is no dunderhead. He thinks. Like now!

The half-grin crept slowly across his face, transforming it, adding a touch of boyish charm. There was a jigsaw puzzle, and he had just fitted in an unusual piece.

'Yes,' he chuckled, 'and telephones get listed, and names get assigned, and get published in telephone books. Right?'

She fought back at him. 'Not always,' she offered sarcastically. 'A little more money makes it an unlisted number. All it takes is money.'

'Interesting problem,' he mused. 'But we'll come to that later. Look, my problem is very simple. I'm down here temporarily doing work in connection with the DEA—the Drug Enforcement Agency. Certain people in the business on the other side have decided to make a political statement, like burning down my house. Like sending a hit squad to remove me from the scene. We think we've caught up with all of them, but you never know. So I want one more day of isolation, and then we'll be in the clear.'

'A hit squad?'

'An assassination team,' he explained. 'It's a complicated world. We've stirred up a fuss in the Columbian drug trade, so they hired an international hit squad to get after us. It gets a little hard to take, I know, but it happens.'

'Well!' Suddenly out of breath, Penny collapsed into a chair. 'I—that's hard to believe. Not right here on the Cape. That couldn't be!'

'Believe it,' he returned. 'It happens more times than I want to admit. Drug-running is a big business, and a little murder on the side is hardly important to the big ones. Now you see why I don't want Abby out in public?'

'Yes,' she sighed. 'I—I see. I find it hard to believe, but I see.' What she saw, but didn't want to tell him, was that she was not all that sure which side of the drug-smuggling business he was in. Which isn't exactly the kind of statement you make to a powerfully built man who is sitting in your kitchen, and with no help available for miles around. Not at all. Penny Harris had been raised in a peculiar society, but she had spent enough time hiding to become streetwise. 'Then since you're here,' she told him, 'you could perhaps take back your daughter, and I'll go shopping by myself.'

'Aw, but that's no fun for me,' Abby mourned.

'Shut up,' her father snapped.

'Don't talk to *any* child that way,' Penny said angrily, 'and particularly not *this* one.'

'And why not this one?' he boomed.

'Because Penny likes me,' the little girl interrupted. 'And I like her, too. So there!'

'And that's no way to talk to your father,' Penny snapped, forgetting for the moment whose side she was on. Frank Corey laughed, and after a moment of stunned surprise, his daughter joined in.

'And that's *not* funny,' Penny gasped. There was the tiniest tear forming in the corner of her eye. Rather than let him see and enjoy, she dashed from the room, snatched up her shoulder satchel, and slammed the front door behind her.

She slammed the van door behind her too, coaxed the engine to sputter and start, and drove off in a cloud of dust and a squeal of tyres. She was still talking to herself when she reached the junction of Route 132. A cerulean TransAm whistled by her at that point, sounding its horn like a challenge. The noise brought her back down to earth, and she concentrated on her driving for the rest of the trip.

Her reform did not stretch beyond driving the van, however. Behind the shopping cart, as she roamed through the food warehouse, a face kept getting in her way. Frank Corey. What a strange man. Devil or hero? Lawyer or gangster? Homely or—well, he wasn't all that ugly after all, was he? Maybe it was the light, that first day. Or the fact that she was so tired. Not handsome, of course. What *was* it that bothered her?

Her memory, searching, found its target. Twelve years ago—or thirteen? When, for a brief month, her Aunt Margaret came into Grandfather's house, and took a little lost girl under her wing. A little girl who was trying so hard to be a boy and win Grandfather's approval. And for that short month she had been a *real* girl, with brushed hair, and dresses that fitted, and stories at bedtime. 'Hidden treasures,' Aunt Margaret had said. They had been reading *Beauty and the Beast*. 'Beauty isn't skin deep,' her aunt had insisted. 'It's not even at skin level. Beauty is deep down, down in the heart. It's like a golden lode that you have to dig out. There's no magic involved. Beauty is always there, like a hidden treasure. You just have to find it.'

The idea followed her all the way back to Navigation Lane. So strong was it, that when he came out to help her carry the stacked grocery bags into the house, she had this mad urge to see for herself!

And by the time they had finished the job, stacked the food away in its proper containers and then straightened up the kitchen, the thought had grown to monstrous proportions. He stood in the centre of the kitchen, folding the paper bags in which the food had been packed. 'Something is on your mind,' he said. A statement, not a question.

'Yes,' she agreed.

'Well, out with it. If it's all that funny I could use a laugh myself.'

'I—I think perhaps you wouldn't see any humour in it,' she stalled.

'You'll never know until you try,' he grinned back at her. 'I've been known to laugh at things from time to time.'

'You promise you won't be mad?'

'Oh, it's that sort of a joke?'

'Yes.' A very meek yes. In fact, one could call it a very half-hearted 'yes'.

'Okay, I'll go along with the gag. I solemnly promise that I'll not be angry at whatever it is.'

She studied his face, an inch by inch scan. 'Close your eyes,' she commanded. He shrugged his shoulders and complied. She stepped closer, continuing her survey. He opened one eye. 'I don't really have all day,' he suggested.

'The eyes,' she demanded. 'Close your eyes.' He grinned that half-smile down at her, and closed both eyes. Pluck up a little courage, she told herself. You'll never know if you don't try. Do you want to know? Of course I do, she assured herself. She moved another step closer, brushing up against him, feeling the strength of his chest pressing against her excited breasts. Of course I want to know! Both hands snaked up around his neck, twisting in his soft hair. There was an electric feeling, as if she were about to touch a high-voltage wire. He stood like a statue. Up on tiptoes, pulling him down slightly, she kissed him gently. It was the first time in her life she had ever initiated a kiss, and she was not at all sure what the results might be. Pleasant, certainly. He didn't taste like stale cigarette smoke, or peppermint candy. He tasted—just nice. Warm, moist, interesting.

It was all so interesting that when his arms moved to surround her, and squeeze her more strongly up against his iron frame, she was caught by surprise. She half-opened her mouth to protest, and that seemed to be the end of the game they were playing. Control passed out of her hands with such ease that she hardly knew what to do next. Luckily, he did.

Her world changed. The warmth, the gentleness, all fled before the onslaught of emotions she had read about but never expected to feel. Riots of sensation. Strange flaming signals from all her centres of sexuality. From all those places which had failed in their reporting services throughout all the twenty years of her life that were past. And the feelings kept on and on as one of his arms roamed up and down her spine, caressing, teasing, stroking. It lasted until, breathless, she found him pushing her slightly away.

She kept her eyes down, trying to hide her emotions behind her long curly lashes, until she regained control of her breathing apparatus. Her knees felt a wondering weakness; so much so that she clutched at his forearms to keep herself upright. And only then, when she had mastered herself, did she look up at him. There was a surprised look on his face—a look of, well, it just had to be enjoyment. And, for just a flashing moment, she swore to herself late that night, an aura of—good Lord—handsomeness!

'And what does all that prove?' he asked quietly. If I didn't know better I would swear he's having trouble breathing, she told herself. What was that all about? Lord, I forget what it was all about. What?

'I can't for the life of me remember,' she sighed. 'Would you like some lunch?' He would.

It was after lunch that things changed. They dined on tomato soup and toasted cheese sandwiches, which Abby pronounced to be the best food she had ever had.

'Hardly that,' her father said quellingly. Penny's smile of thanks had started. She wiped it off instantly. 'But certainly it ranks up among the best two or three meals we've ever had,' he continued. Penny sat there blushing, unable to add a Yea or Nay to the conversation.

'Our chef is struck dumb,' he laughed. 'Come on, Abby, let's sneak outside for some sunshine before she recovers and makes us do the dishes.'

'And why would I want him to do that?' she asked herself as she sat quite still, half in a daze. It took a determined effort to finally hoist herself up and start on the dishes by herself.

It can hardly take an hour to wash three bowls, three spoons and a griddle, but it did. She was still daydreaming, her hands in the cold dish water, when he burst back in on her.

'Do you have a pair of binoculars?' he asked brusquely.

'Who me? Binoculars? That ranks way up there with telephones,' she told him. It was hard to avoid a certain coolness in her voice. He had jostled her out of the depths of a magnificently warm and entrancing daydream, one that she hated to leave for the cold world of dirty dishes and binoculars. But the way he had asked the question worried her. 'There's some trouble?' she questioned weakly.

'I'm not sure,' he returned. 'But when I'm not sure I always adopt the conclusion that we've got trouble.'

'What kind?'

He waved a map he held in his hand towards the harbour, and the high dunes that made up Sandy Neck, across the way. 'There's somebody over there on the Neck,' he said slowly. 'Someone who seems to be interested in what's going on over on this side of the world. Somebody who is watching us with binoculars.'

'But how in the world can you know that?' she asked.

'Because the sun's sparkling off the lenses of his glasses,' he answered. 'Whoever it is hasn't had much experience in sneaking around with binoculars.' He rested one hand on her shoulder and could feel the trembling shivers that were shaking her. 'Hey, don't take it all that seriously,' he consoled. 'According to my map he might not be watching us—he might very well be watching anything from Salt Meadow Lane to Packet Landing Lane. Were you expecting someone to drop in?'

'Yes,' she whispered. 'Some day.'

'Don't be alarmed.' He pulled her hard up against him with both hands. She went willingly, resting her head on the soft weave of his sweater.

'I—I can't help it,' she sighed. 'I've been expecting somebody—somewhere—for the past six months. But I had hoped that they—well—I had hoped that they wouldn't come until January—or February, and now they're here!'

It was almost impossible to keep the tears back. She let the floodgates go. He held her warmly, comfortingly, saying not a word until the flow had passed its peak. 'Maybe it's not what you think,' he said. 'Don't let it worry you. I'll take some steps.'

'What could you do?' she asked bitterly.

'And don't worry your head about that, either,' he chuckled. She could feel the warmth of his fingers coiling through her loose hair. 'Don't worry about a thing, little love. I think I'll just go over there and make whoever it is an offer they can't refuse. Will you watch out for Abby for a little while?'

She nodded dumbly at him, and watched as he hitched up his slacks and started out the door. Little love? she thought. I don't know how long it's been since anyone called me little. And love? I wonder if he knew what he was saying. Maybe it's just one of those popular buzz-words that people use these days. But it did sound nice, didn't it? And that other—I'll make them an offer they can't refuse. *That* she recognised. So did everyone else who watched detective movies or read the papers. 'Oh Lord, what have I got myself into?'

But, putting her fears behind her, she mustered up enough courage to go out into the postage-stamp back yard to sit and talk with Abby while her father rattled up the track towards Route 6A.

CHAPTER THREE

HE didn't return until well into the evening. Abby had been so tired, and the house next door looked so empty, so derelict, that Penny took her upstairs and tucked her into one of the twin beds. The child was asleep before Penny had finished two pages of *The Scarecrow of Romney Marsh*. She tiptoed down the stairs, leaving the bedroom door open just in case Abby woke up to a strange night.

The day had ended in a blaze of glory, with the sun setting behind the rim of clouds just over Plymouth. Long scarlet fingers of light touched the water of the bay, and disappeared. Venus hung bright in the sky, chasing the moon. The Great Marsh was quiet, the seagulls nesting, the swallows making their last flocked pass over the wide marshlands. Only a trickling of water down into the several little streams that drained the area at low tide could be heard. The odour of ozone filled her lungs.

Penny took in the beauty of it all, wishing. The night air was chilled. She went back in for her windbreaker, picked up her only folding lounge chair, and went out into the back yard. She was still there, entranced, when he drove up. She heard him knock on the front door, but was too lazy to move. Moments later he came round the house, surprised to see her stretched out on the lounge.

'Abby?' he asked.

'Upstairs in my bedroom,' she answered. 'She's asleep already. I didn't know when you would be back, and it didn't seem right to leave her all alone in that empty house. I'd offer you a chair, but I only own this one.' And then her conscience bothered her. 'Would you like a cup of coffee? Instant, of course.'

'Of course,' he chuckled, and then grew serious. 'You and I have some talking to do,' he said. 'A good cup of coffee might make it all easier. Need a hand up?'

Without thinking she extended a hand, and he gently pulled her to her feet. She led the way into the kitchen, and put the kettle on. He closed and locked the back door. 'Surely it's not *that* bad?' she enquired.

'Oh, you mean the door? Force of habit, I suppose. We never did bother with locking up at home, but in the three months I've been down here—well, it's better this way.' He pulled out one of the kitchen chairs and sat down. Her hands were busy with the spoon and coffee, all familiar tasks, but her mind kept churning. He looked—changed. It was hard to say in what manner. His face was lined and grim, but there was something different. Trouble? Was it true that someone had been watching them—her—with binoculars? And if so, who? Or more importantly, why? Her hands trembled, scattering a spray of coffee granules over the work area next to the sink. She bit at her lip to restore calm. It was necessary to be calm if she were to face him this night. She could almost feel the spurt of adrenalin pumping through her system. As soon as the two mugs were filled she transferred them to the table and took a seat across from him. 'Well?'

'Well what?' He sipped at the coffee, taking care not to burn his lip.

'Well, you were gone a long time,' she sighed. Damn the man! He's going out of his way to be hard to get along with. 'Surely you found out something, or did something or talked to somebody?'

'All of the above,' he commented, 'and as soon as I get a lip safely over the edge of this mug I'll tell you all about it.' He tested the coffee, meditated, and finally set the mug to one side.

'First of all,' he said, 'our troubles—Abby's and mine—seem to be over. The FBI is positive it's got a hand on all the members of the hit team. So that's one bit of good news.' He went back to his mug for another sip.

'Then I suppose you'll be wanting to move out of this slum district,' she sighed, hardly able to keep her upper lip from quivering. It had been bad enough when he and his daughter had moved into her splendid isolation, and now it was equally bad to think that they would be leaving. Why it made a difference she could not explain, but it did.

'No, we don't intend to move out for a while,' he said. 'Abby likes it here.'

'Well, I surely don't know why,' Penny snapped. 'You never let her go out of the area. It's almost as if she were in jail or something.'

'Don't dramatise,' he returned. 'I come from a family of great actors, I don't need another one. Who's Henry Francis?'

There was nothing he could have said that guaranteed her attention more than that simple query.

'Why—why would you want to know?' she stammered.

'He *is* somebody you know?'

'I—yes.'

'That's all? Just yes?'

'Yes.' She squeezed her hands together hard to stop the trembling.

'Look, it may be hard to believe,' he said, 'but I'm actually trying to help. I'm on your side. Now, who is Henry Francis?'

'I—he—my Uncle Henry. Well, not exactly my uncle. He's a distant cousin of my mother. Where did you hear the name? Dear God, tell me before I fall on the floor in little pieces!' She pushed back her chair and stood up. Fear and anger held equal sway. She raised both hands, fists doubled, as if to threaten him, and then thought better of it, and pressed them into her breasts. He shook his head in disgust.

'Don't make a big thing out of it,' he offered softly. He came around the table. Before she recognised what was going on she was surrounded by those arms again, her cheek pressed into his soft sweater. The warmth, the assurance, the dependability of him, all worked together to quell her fears. 'Tell me about it,' he murmured into her hair.

The long stranglehold she had maintained on her tongue evaporated under his urging. She relaxed completely for the first time in over a year. 'It all started a long time ago,' she sighed. 'My grandfather made a fortune on the stock market. He—I was his only grandchild. My father died in the war before I was born, my mother when I was born. There wasn't anybody else, just Grandfather. He took me in and raised me. But he wanted a boy, you know, and he treated me like a boy. My little Penn, he would call me. But then—I—grew up, you see, and by the time I was twelve he couldn't deceive himself any longer, and—well—he spent most of his time making more money. And then he died. I was fifteen then. It was a very lonely time, but when Uncle Henry came to live with me—I wished I could be lonely again! But the money——'

'But the money?'

'Grandfather didn't leave the money to Uncle Henry—or to me, for that matter. He left it all to the Philip Harris Foundation. Forty million dollars. The money earned by investing was supposed to go to worthwhile charities. Uncle Henry, as my guardian, controls the Foundation until my twenty-first birthday, according to Grandfather's will. And then I—I was supposed to take over.'

'So what happened?'

'I—I think Grandfather trained me too well when he was treating me as a boy. I kept going down to the Foundation offices and asking questions, and——'

'And?'

'And Uncle Henry made me stop. He said I had no head for business, and he talked about sending me off to school to train as a librarian. Me, would you believe it, a librarian?'

'I believe it,' he commented. 'It takes five years. You have to have a Master's degree. Then what?'

'Then I graduated from High School and refused to go to college. Uncle Henry and I had all kinds of arguments. I demanded a job at the Foundation. He finally found me one, down in the computer room.'

'Computers? You like computer work?'

'Yes. I became a *hacker* when I was thirteen years old.'

'A hacker? Oh, one of those smart kids who get their kicks from breaking into other people's computer memories?'

'There's nothing dishonest about it,' she snapped at him. 'It's all perfectly legal. People who don't want to share their computer memories have the choice of developing a foolproof code system, or simply disconnecting the telephone lines from their computer. It's just a game, that's all.'

'And you broke into the Foundation's secret system?'

'I didn't *break in*,' she snapped. 'I just—happened to deduce the entry code. But eventually they found out.'

'And then what happened?'

'I was twenty years old by that time, and one morning I was late getting to work, and as I walked down the corridor at home I heard Uncle Henry in the library talking on the telephone, and he mentioned my name, so I just couldn't help stopping to listen. You *do* understand?'

'Yes, I understand, Penny.' He said it with a perfectly straight face, but she could hear the laughter behind the words. She pushed herself away from him and stalked towards the kitchen door. 'Hey now, Penny,' he called after her.

She stopped and glared over her shoulder. 'The last thing in the world I need,' she said fiercely, 'is another smart-mouth in my life. Are you going to take your daughter home with you? And please don't slam the door as you go out!'

She was pleased with her exit-line, but unfortunately she could not get offstage quickly enough. He caught up with her with ridiculous ease, and terminated her flight by putting his hands on her shoulders and turning her round.

'I went round to Sandy Neck,' he said quietly, 'with a couple of my friends. And who do you guess we found snooping around in the sand?'

'I haven't the slightest idea,' she returned coldly, 'and I don't think I really want to know, but you're going to tell me anyway, aren't you?'

'I'm afraid that's just what I'm going to do.' He said it mournfully, but she knew very well he was faking it.

'Then say it and get it over with,' she snapped. 'I'm tired and I need to get to bed.'

'What? After loafing around all day?' She gave him one of her patented 'turn off' looks, but he was totally unimpressed. 'So, as I said, I picked up a couple of my friends and went over to Sandy Neck. And there, nestling in a hollow in the sand dunes, we came across a Mr Patrick Muldoon. You know Mr Muldoon?'

'I've never heard of him. Are you finished?' She essayed a yawn, but it was hard to sustain. 'So who is he?'

'Mr Muldoon is a private detective from Boston. This coffee is getting cold. Could we have another?'

'Don't stall,' she snarled at him. She leaned across the table in her excitement, and glared at him.

'Hmm. Green eyes,' he chuckled. 'I've not caught you in the light before. Nice. I like green eyes.'

'Mr Muldoon,' she snapped. 'Well?'

'You know, I do believe I'm getting hungry,' he sighed. 'You went shopping, didn't you? How about a nice Western omelette, or something simple like that?'

'I'll give you something simple,' she raged. 'Right on your head I'll give it. You don't get a single thing more in this house until I've heard about Mr Muldoon!' She jumped to her feet and snatched at the handle of the griddle, which had been sitting peacefully on top of the gas stove.

'All right, all right,' he said. 'Put down the weapon and we'll talk about your Mr Muldoon!'

'He's not *my* Mr Muldoon!' she shouted at him. Her hand wavered from lack of choice, but finally she set the griddle back down on the stove top.

'Our Mr Muldoon then,' he substituted. 'A fine young man with a large pair of binoculars and a zoom-lens camera. After a little persuasion our Mr Muldoon spoke freely.'

'I'll bet he did,' she mumbled. 'You made him an offer he couldn't refuse!'

'Exactly!' He beamed at her, like a teacher who had finally got the right answer from a slow student. 'Exactly. He confided in us. It seems that he was hired by a Mr Henry Francis to locate his lost niece, a Miss Penelope Bloom Harris. You've been telling us a fib, haven't you, Miss—er—Bloom?'

She blushed and dropped her eyes.

'So it seemed that Mr Muldoon had been successful! Fortunately, he had not yet mailed off his first report to Boston, so I'm afraid that Mr Henry Francis still doesn't know where you are.'

She blanched. I'm not afraid of Uncle Henry, she told herself determinedly. I'm not! But I *am* afraid of what he might do if he gets his hands on me. She swayed under the impact of her confused emotions. Frank Corey reached out a hand to steady her, and then directed her back to her chair. She sat down, a glum expression on her face.

'Now then,' he continued. 'You were saying about your childhood and your grandfather, and lots of money, and your so-called uncle. And then you broke the code at the Foundation and entered the computer and found out something. What?'

'I—they—none of the money was going to charity. They were using it all for themselves. Uncle Henry, Cousin Oscar, and all their little relatives. Not a penny to charity in the past three years. Not a penny!'

'Ah,' he hissed, 'that's what it's all about. And then one day you were late for work, and you came down the hall—where?'

'In Grandfather's house, on Gainsborough Street in

Boston. I had always lived there, and then Uncle Henry moved in, and Oscar, and then a whole pack of others.'

'Cousin Oscar?'

'A distant cousin, many times removed. Uncle Henry wanted me to marry him, but I just couldn't. I didn't even like him.'

'So that brings us back to the story. You were hurrying down the hall, and you heard your uncle on the telephone, and he mentioned your name, so you listened. Just what did he say?'

'It—it was my birthday, you understand.' She was talking so softly that he moved his chair closer to hear. 'It was my twentieth birthday, and I was feeling on top of the world, and then I heard him say my name, so I stopped to listen.'

'And?'

'He said—*and maybe we wouldn't have to worry about audits and inspections and all that if Penelope never gets to be twenty-one!*'

She could hear his breath hiss inward between clenched teeth. That cold look flashed in his eyes again. Suddenly they were back to square one again. He was a strong, ugly man thinking ugly thoughts. Her tears came; not a flood, just a silent trickle. Not out of fear, she told herself. Not out of remembrance of what Uncle Henry had said, but because she had lost something in Frank—some gentleness, some inward beauty which had just been knocked out. Something in him she had come to care a great deal about, and had not recognised until just that moment, when it was gone. She used the back of one knuckle to clear her eyes.

'And that's when you ran?'

'Yes. That's when I ran. I've thought about it a great deal in the last nine months. Sometimes I think it couldn't have been real—that I must have imagined it all. But I—on that day, all I could think about was that I was twenty, and there was forty million dollars. I think Uncle Henry would do a great deal just to continue having that amount of money.'

'So would a great many other people,' he commented. 'And that's what you've been doing? Avoiding Uncle Henry until you get to be twenty-one? How soon is that?'

'Next January,' she sighed. 'January the twenty-fourth. I thought that—if I were only able to—avoid any accidents until then, that maybe I could take over the Foundation and set things straight.' She smiled weakly at him through the screen of her hair, which had fallen completely down, and hung across her face. He reached over the table and flicked her screen away.

'And do you suppose,' he said wryly, 'that having planned to knock you off before your birthday, he would hesitate to do it after?'

Her heart fell down into her stomach. 'No,' she whispered, 'I never ever thought of that.'

'Well, think about it now. Who gets the money if you die after your birthday?'

'I—don't know,' she stammered. 'I just—never thought——'

'Your grandfather's will never mentioned the subject?'

'Not that I know of. Not in his will, anyway.'

'Then when everything comes to you, I suppose you've made a will?'

'Why no, why should I? I'm only——'

'Being only twenty doesn't mean you'll live for ever,' he said calmly. 'So you have no will. And who is your closest relative?'

'I—why, Uncle Henry, I suppose.'

'Of course,' he sighed.

'I don't know what you mean,' she complained. 'I just don't understand you. Well, I don't!'

He sat there and grinned at her, that crazy one-sided grin that was so attractive. She was almost mesmerised by it. His voice faded into the background as she studied the crags and crannies of him. Unconsciously one of her hands crossed the table and stroked back the hank of hair that had slipped down over his forehead.

A snapping noise brought her back to the present. He was snapping his fingers under her nose and grinning, a great full-faced grin.

'You haven't heard a word I've said, have you?'

'Hmmmm?' she asked. A blush spread across her sun-darkened face, running up from her throat to her ears.

'I said that things won't improve for you before or after your birthday. That is, if your Uncle Henry is as mean as you suggest. Let me give you some legal advice.'

'If it costs anything, I can't afford it,' she snapped.

'You can afford it,' he laughed. 'It's free. Make yourself a will, and make sure that your Uncle Henry gets a copy of it. Don't leave *anything* to him!'

'Now why didn't *I* think of that?' she asked. 'You really *are* a lawyer? I never really thought lawyers were smart. Clever, yes, but not smart.'

'I'll be darned,' he said. 'A real genuine compliment. That *is* what it was, wasn't it?'

'Yes,' she answered, 'and I meant it. But you didn't answer my question, did you?'

He waved a hand vaguely, as if her question had no importance in the scheme of things. 'Tell me then,' he continued. 'What would happen if you got married?'

'That's not likely,' she returned. 'A girl still has to wait to be asked. And nobody's asking. Nobody.'

'Blind,' he snorted. 'Wherever you've been living they're all blind. But that's not what I was asking. Doesn't your grandfather's will make some mention of marriage? They usually do, you know.'

'I haven't any idea,' she said. 'It all happened so long ago, and I was only fifteen. I don't remember.'

'Too bad. If you were married, your husband and children would automatically displace your uncle from any inheritance.'

'That would be nice. Can you imagine the vine-covered cottage and children bit for me? Not a chance.'

'You would like to be married, Penny?'

'Very much,' she sighed. 'Doesn't every woman? But nobody wants to marry a giant.'

'And children? Would you like to have your own children?'

'Of course I would. I've always dreamed of that. Two or three at least. Or maybe four. But you can see it's all a dream. I've no experience with children, there never were any around our house except me. And no happy husbands, or mothers to be a role model for me. Nothing. Oh, don't misunderstand me. When I was young I had a great deal of fun. Grandpa took me every place and showed me everything—up until he could no longer pretend that I was a boy. And it's been all downhill since then. What are you doing?'

He was pulling her to her feet, wrapping one arm around her shoulders, and leading her out of the house into the back yard. The moon was still high, not quite full, but silvery brilliant, splattering light across the salt marshes at their feet. His arm drew her closer, until her head was resting on his shoulder.

'The moonlight looks like fairy paths,' she murmured. 'I look at them and think how easy it would be to dance across the Marsh on them, never touching a foot to anything but moonlight.' He squeezed her gently in acknowledgement.

'So I've got a romantic here, underneath all those muscles? If you slipped off your moonbeam you'd be up to your neck in water!'

'And I suppose you're one of those pragmatic types,' she accused. 'Well, for your information, Frank Corey, I have very good balance, and probably could run across the Marsh twice to your once.'

'If you're trying to dare me to a race,' he chuckled, 'you've got the wrong man. I never rush in where fools fear to tread. Is that the right quotation?'

'It's a quotation,' she returned sarcastically, 'but I wouldn't guarantee that it's the right one.'

'Sarcasm? I know how to treat that, lady.' He pulled her around to face him, pressed her up against his front, and bent down just enough to caress her lips with his. Just a tender quick salute that had all of pleasure in it, and no pain. She sighed contentedly. He took it for an invitation, and repeated. Just a soft fleeting touch, nothing more.

When he released her she stepped back slightly, then moved to his side, hugging his right arm for support. She looked up and traced the stars. The Big Dipper was upside down, its leading edge pointed towards dim Polaris. Orion the Hunter held centre stage, the stars in his sword belt big and brilliant. 'What does he hunt?' she half-whispered.

'I don't know,' he whispered back. 'I'm too busy with my *own* hunting.' She pushed away from him. 'All you men are alike, aren't you!' But the scene and its dreaming quality were broken. She felt almost as if she *had* danced across the Marsh on moonbeams—and had fallen off. She shivered, but not from the cold.

'You never did decide about Abby,' she mentioned. 'Does she stay the night, or go home with you?'

'Which would you prefer?' he offered. He was no longer looking at her. He had turned towards the ocean and, hands in his pockets, was whistling an unrecognisable tune. It seemed to have only three notes. There was no way she could see his face clearly, but the furrows were plain on his forehead. Thinking? Or regretting? Or maybe even remembering? Abby had a mother. She must have been beautiful to produce a child like Abigail. Was he thinking of that now, here in the clear Cape moonlight? It was an idea that she didn't want to think about. Not that there was anything in the situation that was any of Penny Harris's business. None at all. So why did it bother her?

'I think we ought to leave her where she is,' she said calmly. 'She's a big girl and moving her now would surely wake her up.'

'What?' So he *had* been miles away! And that's why I won't ever get married, Penny told herself woefully. Here I am in a lonely spot with a fine man, plenty of moonlight, and wearing my best perfume, and I can't even keep his attention!

'I said we ought to leave Abby where she is for the night. She might wake up if we try to move her.'

'Yes.' Now that's a great answer, full of love and passion! The thought was enough to trigger her laughter—at herself. He was still staring off into the distance. She coughed to clear her throat and stood silently behind him, waiting. For what? She had not a single idea in her head. Some nice safe subject to talk about? Something left unexplained. Yes! She tugged at the sleeve of his sweater and he turned around.

'That man—Mr Muldoon, the detective. You said he hadn't notified my uncle. But I suppose he will pretty soon?'

'I don't think so,' he returned. 'I think we persuaded him to drop the case.'

'You said he wasn't a very big man. You didn't hurt him, did you?'

'Me? I never laid a finger on him, Penny. I just reasoned with him. He agreed very quickly with the Sheriff and me.'

'The Sheriff?' Her mouth fell open. Things were getting more confusing than ever.

'Yes, and one of his Deputies. Do you worry about everyone who spies on you?'

'Well, I can't help that. I was raised a Christian, and I believe in certain moralities!'

'Is that what you plan with Uncle Henry? Turn the other cheek?'

'I—I don't know that I could go *that* far,' she sighed. 'I try to do the best that I can, but that doesn't mean I follow all the precepts of the Church all the time. I—I think I'd better go in now. It's late. Can I take Abby shopping tomorrow?'

'Any place you want,' he chuckled. 'She's out of prison, and we *are* going to stay in this neighbourhood. I appreciate what you're doing for me with Abby.'

'For *Abby* I'd be willing to do most anything!' And

why do I sound so prim and prissy, she asked herself. I'm not one of those dainty and demure little misses!

'Don't worry, I heard the emphasis,' he laughed. 'You must be tired, love. All the Crusader spirit has gone out of you.'

'You don't have to overwhelm me with your education,' she snapped. 'So I never did get to college. At least I know you can't outfit a little girl with one twenty-dollar bill. She needs a whole new wardrobe. And that, Mr Corey, will set you back ten or fifteen of those twenty-dollar bills.'

'I hear you,' he returned. She could see his shadowed frame fishing in one of his pockets, pulling out a wallet, counting off fifteen bills.

'How do you know they're all twenties?' she gulped.

'Because that's all I carry,' he answered. 'Here.'

'I don't have any pockets,' she stammered.

'What do you know,' he said happily. 'I've wanted to do this for the longest time!' He caught one of her hands and pulled her close. She watched, dazed. His other hand tugged open her jacket, unfastened the top four buttons of her blouse, and tucked the money in one huge wad into the top of her bra. 'Man, there's hardly room here at all,' he said, suddenly solemn. 'You are a whole lot of woman, Penny Harris.'

Her reaction was slow, confused. Her free hand came up quickly to her breast, and landed on top of his. Instead of prying him off, scratching him silly, forcing him to withdraw, her hand was holding his in place, feeling the rough warmth of him on the upper curve of her breast, striving to hold on to the minute, the excitement, the strange emotion. The tableau held for a moment. He terminated it all, lifting his hand gently, refastening the buttons, pulling her jacket closed and zipping it up to her chin. She stood frozen in place, unable to move a foot.

When he finished the task his hands came back to her shoulders. 'Good night, little love,' he said softly, and once again those predatory lips swept across hers, and then returned to bury her senses in sweet longing. She clung to him, arms around his neck, pressing herself against him until he broke contact again, stepped back a pace or two, and repeated his good night.

'You must think I'm some sort of a pushover,' she said bitterly.

'I know better than that,' he rumbled. 'If only you weren't so filthy rich!'

She almost missed those final words. He had his back to her, and was walking across the yard. She stood there until he was out of sight. Until the front door of his house banged behind him, and a light came on in his living-room. With that she broke out of her daze, forced herself indoors, and upstairs for a quick shower.

'What do you suppose he meant by that?' she asked the shower head, the towel rack, the floor mat, and got not a single answer. She was still asking as she took off her shower cap, rubbed herself down briskly with an extra-large towel, and slipped into her nightgown. Why did he kiss me? Or why did he——Even in the shelter of her own bathroom she could not bring herself to say the words. But she did stop long enough in front of the full-length mirror hung on the back of the bathroom door to examine herself. She stood sidewise and cupped her own breasts, one in each hand. Why? There was no answer. She crept quietly into the bedroom so as not to disturb the child in the other bed, and buried herself under the blankets.

It was a long and sleepless night, full of tossing and turning. How in the world can a girl get a good night's sleep when every time she closes her eyes that man is there, staring at her?

CHAPTER FOUR

MORNING came before she was ready for it, like a gold and red explosion through the two east windows. The bed next to her was empty. She yawned, stretched, and brushed her hair out of her eyes before mustering up the willpower to climb out of the warm bed.

It took long minutes under the cold shower to bring her completely round. There was a problem for today. Lord, there were always problems, on whatever *today* it happened to be. But this one was—Abby, and those ridiculous clothes she wore? Not exactly. But her father—now that was what you could call a man-sized problem! And what the devil do you intend to do about it, Miss Penelope Harris? That face of his was hiding in her mind, just out of reach. Hiding, waiting to jump out at her whenever she relaxed.

'I just don't have the experience,' she thought as she turned up the cold water. It sent shivers down her spine; but then, so did he. Damn the man! There's only one real solution, she thought. One that her grandfather had taught her. 'Most problems, if you just leave them strictly alone, will go away of their own accord!'

With that intention she mustered up a pair of bright red jeans, a yellow blouse, and a pair of blue socks, and set out to face the day. Abby was in the kitchen when she came downstairs, busily munching on a bowl of cornflakes. The little girl managed a smile around the edges of a full mouth.

'Eat hearty, girl,' Penny told her. 'Today we go shopping for clothes—for you. I can't bear to see you spend another day with that crazy outfit of yours.'

Abby swallowed excitedly. 'You mean you're gonna buy me some clothes?'

53

'Well, your Dad is paying, so we might as well go first class!'

'That's what Grandma always says,' Abby returned. 'Only she laughs when she says it. And Granpa, he makes funny noises, like something hurts him.'

'You don't say,' Penny returned absentmindedly as she pottered around making coffee, and gathering up the shreds of what would be her own breakfast. And then it struck her. This little girl could be a gold mine of information, just waiting for the right questions!

'Your dad's mother and father?' she asked casually.

'Oh yes.' The words were muffled under the crunch of breakfast food. 'Grandma Corey.'

'Where do they live, Abby? Not around here, I guess?'

'No, they live a long ways off, in Northampton. I would've stayed with Grandma when Papa had this assignment down here, but she's been sick with the flu, and Uncle George works in Springfield, and Uncle Harry had to go to Europe, and Aunt Ethel is still in college you know, and Marion is in the hospital. They just got a new baby, Uncle Harry and Aunt Marion, did you know that? Only it's another girl. Grandma wants a boy!'

Oh wow, she thought. The man has more family than good looks. And if that's the case, why is he hanging around in a slum district like Navigation Lane? What sort of a job could have brought him down from the hills? Drugs, he said something about drugs. My brain keeps going in circles. I can't seem to remember what the devil he's been saying to me. Every time he starts talking I seem to get buried in daydreams.

'No, I didn't know that,' she answered. The egg in the frying pan spat at her, and she rushed to turn down the heat. One egg, two pieces of toast, a glass of orange juice, and three mugs of coffee—not all at once. That constituted her normal breakfast. She loaded the plate and mug, and set them down on the table.

'You cook nice,' Abby offered.

'Yes, don't I,' Penny laughed. 'Anything, so long as it's eggs or comes in a can. I make a mean cup of coffee too, just so long as it's instant. Are you a good cook?'

'I ain't yet, but Grandma is teaching me. Hey, look, it's Dad.'

As indeed it was. Barging in through the kitchen door as if it were *his* house, kissing the little girl, and patting Penny in an entirely objectionable place, and then sitting down at the table in *her* chair.

'Thank you,' he managed, as he picked up a fork and demolished the egg. 'Although to tell the truth I prefer three eggs for breakfast, and a strip or two of bacon to go with it. The toast is nice, though.'

'Well, I'm just glad it all meets your requirements,' she snapped at him. 'In case anyone wants to know, that was *my* breakfast.'

'And now it's all gone,' Abby mourned. 'Just like Goldilocks and the three bears, ain't it?'

'Isn't it,' Penny corrected. 'And yes, it is!'

'Oh, did I make a mistake?' he asked.

She wondered whether it would be worth her while to walk around the table and box his ears, or perhaps even worse punishment, kiss him? But she hadn't the courage for it, not in broad daylight, with his daughter looking on. And besides, her hands had automatically cracked two more eggs in the pan. There wasn't any bacon, but she made a mental note to get some. In the meantime there was the smoked ham? Before she could stabilise her thinking, slices of the ham rested in the griddle beside his eggs, and she was nibbling on a slice of burnt toast. It was something she knew she wouldn't *dare* offer to visitors. She dished it all up with a deep sigh and set it before him.

'Abby, if you've finished eating, scoot upstairs. You need a shower before we go off clothes hunting. Can you work the shower for yourself?'

'Yes, ma'am.' The little girl pushed her plate aside and skipped out of the room.

'I'd better change if I'm going to register her at

school, as well,' Penny murmured, and went after her. In a way it was lucky that she did. Not that Abby needed an ounce of help, but rather because Penny had reached the end of her patience, and could almost predict that the next thing he asked for at her table would be poured over his head. The way he ducked as she went by his chair seemed to indicate that he felt the same.

'Could you do my hair for me like you did yesterday?' Abby asked. 'I like the way you do it. Grandma does it sometimes, but it hurts.'

'Beginner's luck,' Penny told her as she rubbed the child down briskly with a heavy towel. 'Next time I might very well pull all your hair out—no, I'm only joking, love. Come on into my room, and we'll both get our hair done neatly for a change.'

By the time they finished and came down, he had gone, leaving behind the usual note. 'Be back by four-thirty. Have fun.' Sure we will, she told herself determinedly. It should be a lot of fun, spending *your* money! She hurried the child over to a kitchen chair.

'Did your grandmother buy all those clothes you're wearing?' she asked.

'Oh no. All my clothes got burned in the fire. Mrs Crimmons, who was our housekeeper, picked this stuff up for me before she left.' See there, Penny lectured herself. Judging without hearing the evidence. And all the time you blamed *him* for it!

'Then what kind of clothes do you want?'

'You mean I get to choose?'

'If you get to wear, you get to choose,' Penny told her. 'Do you have any preferences?'

'What would Papa say?'

'Did he say he was coming with us?'

'Nope. He don't like to go shopping.'

'Then he doesn't have anything to say, does he?'

'Yeah!' The little girl's face lit up, and then went dark. It was clear that her father's opinion hovered over her, even at a distance.

'Pay him no mind,' Penny urged. 'What do you really like to wear?'

'Jeans,' came the instant return. 'Slacks. Daddy, he wants me to wear dresses all the time. I 'spose it's nice for Sunday or for a party or something, but I don't want to wear them all the time, do I?' The question mark carried just a tiny quaver—an appeal for support.

'No, you won't want to wear dresses all the time,' Penny agreed. 'And I feel exactly the same way. So the answer for us, love, is Sears and Roebuck. See if you can find a light jacket or a sweater.'

The drive took them down Route 6A to its junction with Route 132, at the edge of Barnstable village, where they turned south. 'We have to come back this way,' Penny said. 'Your new school is just over there, up towards the centre of town.'

'School? I don't wanna go to school down here! I thought we were going home to Northampton. I've got a lot of friends back there, and——' The argument went on, displaying a thousand and one reasons why she should not be incarcerated in the Barnstable Elementary School.

'It's not a gaol,' Penny protested, but it was hard to keep the laughter under control. They had just passed under the Midcape highway bridge, and the Mall was just ahead, announced by a straggling line of car dealerships and motels.

'Hah! A lot you know,' the little girl mumbled. 'I went to that school in Falmouth before our house burned down. The teacher was like that Wicked Witch in the Wizard of Oz. No, I don't wanna go to school in Barnstable! And you can't make me. Can you?'

'I guess not,' Penny sighed. 'Only your mother and father could *make* you go.' The right turn into the Mall was coming up, and she concentrated on the road, so she barely heard the child mumble under her breath. She turned into the south parking lot, opposite Sears and Filenés and the New World Bank, and parked the van in the first available spot.

'I didn't hear what you said,' she commented as she set the parking brake. The little girl looked at her with mutiny in her eyes.

'I said,' Abby repeated fiercely, 'I'd even *go* to your darn school if you were my mother!'

'But, Abby,' she started to protest. 'There's your dad to consider, and your grandmother, and——'

'I don't care,' the girl sobbed. 'I want you to be my mother!'

Oh God, Penny groaned to herself, what a mess you've got yourself into this time! 'I—I don't know what to tell you,' she said. 'I—don't have any experience mothering, love. I never even had a mother of my own to show me how. I—just don't think I'd make a very good mother, Abby. I really don't!'

'Don't you even love me a little bit?'

'I love you a great deal, Abigail.'

'Well, that's all it takes! Grandma told me that. All it takes is love!'

Driven into a corner by irrefutable logic, Penny squirmed in her seat. The easiest thing in the world would be to say yes, I'll be your mother. But there's a great deal more to it than that. How can I explain to this tiny thing what I think about her father? Especially when I don't really know myself! And being confused by it all, Penny took the coward's way out. 'That's something you'll have to talk to your father about,' she said.

The shopping trip through Sears had the appearance of a funeral procession for the first five minutes, but after the passing of those first emotions the child was swept up in clothes and choices and excitement. Everything had to be inspected, everything had to be tried on, everything had to be lovingly folded and stored away in plastic shopping bags. Before Penny put her foot down Frank's money had all but evaporated. She was still juggling figures in her head as they stepped out of the store into the bright Cape sunshine, and as a result failed to see the solid figure in front of her until she bounced off him and slipped to one knee.

'Daddy!' Abby screamed. 'What are you doing here, Daddy?'

'Looking for you.' His strong hands on Penny's elbows restored her to her feet. Their parcels were strewn around her, and a taxicab was honking its horn for passage. Penny could feel the pain of a scrape on her knee, but refused to admit it. Instead she glared at Frank as if it were all his fault. The cab driver put his thumb down on his horn and held it there.

Another damn arrogant male, she told herself, and being sick to death of male arrogance, she pulled herself up to her full height and stalked around to the driver's side of the cab, where an open window gave access to a medium-sized but tubby man. She leaned against the door frame and stuck her head inside the cab.

'Didn't your mother ever tell you not to play with your horn in the street?' she asked quietly. 'Or maybe you would like me to shove it up your nose?'

'You and who else?' he retorted belligerently.

'Me, all by myself,' she snarled at him. 'But if I can't manage, my daughter over there will help out.' The cabbie took a quick look out his other window, noticing Abby and the big smiling man who stood beside her.

'Hey,' he said in a much more conciliatory tone, 'I'm sorry, lady. I just thought maybe you didn't notice I wanted to go by.'

'I noticed,' she grated at him. 'And I was hoping you'd like to argue about it. All those karate lessons I took, and I've never really been able to use them!'

'Not on me, lady,' he responded. 'You just take your time. I surely wouldn't want to run over anything—especially of yours. Just take your time, lady.'

She nodded at him, and walked slowly around the cab and back to the pavement. Abby had already recovered some of the parcels. Frank helped her to gather up the rest, moving as slowly as she. When they had all been regathered, they both stepped back on to the pavement, and waved the cab on. The driver shifted into gear and left the vicinity in a great cloud of smoke.

'He really was in a hurry,' Frank said non-committally as they watched the cab swing hard left back to the highway. 'What did you say to him?'

'Who, me?' she grinned. 'I just made him an offer he couldn't refuse!'

'Made you feel better, did it?'

'Immensely.' She looked up at him. That big broad grin was back. For one idiotic moment she had the impulse to grab at him, to throw her arms around his neck and kiss him prettier. And what a stupid idea that is, she told herself mournfully. Kiss him prettier. Handsomer, maybe, but never prettier!

Her thoughts skidded to a halt. She didn't dare to look at him. She took a quick look in both directions, and stepped off the kerb. The Coreys followed, both laughing their fool heads off. By the time she found the van in the crowded parking lot her bad temper had gradually eased off.

As usual, it took more than a minute or two to get the back door of the van unlocked. There was a trick to it. You had to hold the key just right, and jiggle it. She couldn't seem to get the jiggling right. Frank and his daughter were having a heart-to-heart talk, and no matter how she strained Penny could not quite hear what they were talking about. Eventually it broke up and he came over behind her. His hand relieved hers of the key, and in one casual twist the lock was released and the door opened. He helped her pile the packages inside.

'So ask her, Daddy,' the little girl insisted.

'Not now,' her father returned. 'This isn't the right time.'

'Why did you come?' Penny asked.

'I just remembered you said something about school, and knowing how skittish my young lady is about schools, I thought I'd better come by and help out.'

'Oh? You have that kind of job? You work around here?'

'Temporarily,' he returned. 'I share an office in the County Office building, behind the old court house. But not for long. My part of this job is just about to run out.'

'Oh, but I thought you were going to stay on Navigation Lane,' she said. There was no way she could repress the tremor in her voice. 'It's hardly any use getting Abby in school if you're going to—to where-ever it is that you really live. Is it?'

'No, it wouldn't be,' he answered, 'but we're staying a while. On Navigation Lane, that is. Where are you bound now?'

'I thought I'd go across the street to the other Mall. They have a big food market over there. And then, after that, I thought I would start out for the school.'

'Okay. I'll follow along in my car.'

She managed to get the van started at the first attempt, an altogether unusual feat that made her day. Getting across to the other side of the six-lane Route 132 was no child's play. Traffic seemed to be coming from all directions, and a line was growing behind her at the crossing point. She finally resorted to her old standby. As soon as a small opening showed in the traffic she floored her gas pedal and sent the old truck careening across the divided highway like a rocket. There was a multiple squealing of brakes, which she completely ignored. Experience had taught her that nobody in their right mind would dispute a crossing with a van as old and as battered as hers. And so far she had been right.

Once on the other side of the highway there was no problem swinging into the Capetown Mall. This one centred round a large K-Market, and the food warehouse, and then included a dozen smaller stores. Brooks' chemist, Radio Shack, Pearl Vision, Hobbytown—they were all there in a row, ending with, of all things, an office of the State Department of Revenue. 'All of which proves,' she giggled to Abby, 'that they mean to get your money here, one way or another!'

'What are we getting over here?' Abby asked.

'Bacon,' Penny returned. 'I thought I would get some bacon.'

'Oh, do you like bacon, too?' the child asked. 'My dad loves it.'

'I don't like it at all,' Penny sighed. She shook her head in disgust, and fingered her way through her purse and the pockets of her jeans. Oh well, she thought, that's another paving stone in my road of good intentions. She turned on the ignition again, and started out of the parking lot.

'No bacon?' Abby asked. Somehow or another, impossible as it was, the child sounded just like her father.

'No money,' Penny admitted. 'You wouldn't believe it, but I've only got eighty five cents left!'

'I got a dime,' Abby offered.

'Won't do. Bacon costs a lot more than that. We'll have to wait until I can negotiate a loan from my bank.' It wasn't quite a lie. She had more than enough money in the bank to see her through two or three months, but it was all in a savings account, and she would have to go down to Sandwich to get the cash.

Meanwhile she sped back up the highway towards Route 6A at a miraculous forty miles an hour, and kept an eye on the heavy car behind her. She had not paid it any particular attention before, but the dust which had covered it was gone, and the gleaming black Mercedes proclaimed itself for what it was—a rich man's car. Did lawyers make that much money? She thrust the thought firmly out of her mind. It really didn't *matter* what he did for a living.

Her mind was so cluttered that she drove right by the mailbox in the right, the only indicator that the Barnstable Elementary School lay up at the top of the small rise, set back from the road by a good two hundred feet or more, and hidden by a screen of trees and bushes. And then, with the heavy traffic behind her, there was just no place to stop and turn around until she came to the town centre. She pulled off the road just beyond the fire station. The Mercedes came up behind her, and he came strolling over.

'Lost?' he enquired.

'No, not quite,' she returned. 'I overshot the school entrance. You know the town pretty well?'

'Pretty well,' he said. 'I've been over here for two or three weeks. Our main work was done in Falmouth. Funny place.'

'Funny?' She was ready to rise in defence of her favourite village when he modified the statement.

'Funny as in peculiar,' he added. 'Not funny as in ha ha! Take a good look. The centre is stretched along Main Street here. There's a hill to our right, and salt marshes everywhere to the left. There are two streets that go left, across the marshland, until you get to the other half of town, right down on the shore. Some of the houses face the streets, but have their back doors jacked up over the Marsh. If it wasn't for that big sand bar out there, a good neap tide would sweep the place away—yet it's been standing here since 1639.'

'Daddy,' Abby broke in. 'You said she was too rich for our blood. She ain't. We were gonna get some bacon at the food store. She don't like bacon, but she was gonna get some. Only she didn't have any money left. Only eighty-five cents. How could she be too rich? I got a dime, myself. How much do you have?'

'We'll talk about that later,' he said. 'She was going to buy bacon, and she doesn't like bacon?'

'That's right, Daddy. That's *real* funny, ain't it?'

'Isn't it, love. Isn't it! Yes, that's real funny. And we'd better get you down to the school before you forget everything you ever learned.'

'I s'pose you think everything they say in school is right,' his daughter offered very sarcastically. There was a load of resentment behind the words, as if this were a segment of a long-fought battle between them.

'Of course,' he said. 'Everything. Don't you ever doubt it, little girl.'

'And I ain't a little girl,' she grumbled as she sank back into her seat.

It was the work of a moment to retrace their path, locate the proper entryway, and drive up the slight hill to the school. It was a relatively new building, all on one floor, with huge glass windows, well-lighted halls, and a very competent secretary, willing to stop to take care of their needs.

'I think I have all the papers here,' Frank told the middle-aged lady. 'She was last enrolled in Falmouth.' He handed over an envelope of papers. The secretary made some entries, consulted a list, and returned the envelope.

'We have room in Miss Metcalfe's class,' she announced, 'but it's too late for anything today. Perhaps your wife could drive her in for the next two or three days until we get her bus schedule straightened out?'

Abby began to giggle, and Penny turned blush-red. Frank Corey cleared his throat. Both the females waited to hear what he would say. His statement was anti-climactic. 'Yes, of course,' he said. 'I suppose that eventually the bus would pick her up on the highway? I don't suppose they would drive down Navigation Lane?'

'I suspect you're right,' the secretary said. She got up and handed Penny a small slip of paper. It listed the teacher's name and room number. She walked them to the door of her office, where she stopped. 'It's a real pleasure,' she commented, 'to find both parents interested enough to come to register a new student. You are a lucky pair to have such a delightful daughter. And I'll see you tomorrow, Mrs Corey.'

All the way out to the cars Abby had difficulty restraining herself. Her father stalked ahead of them, head high, wearing a fierce mask. Penny followed behind, unable to decide whether to laugh or to cry. It was when they reached the vehicles that Abby cut loose.

'Everything they tell me in school is true. Right, Daddy?'

'Oh, shut up, girl. Don't go around showing off!'

'I only know what my parents tell me. Right, Daddy?'

'Damn it, Miss Harris, will you kindly take this smart kid back home! I've got work to do!'

Trying her best to keep a straight face, Penny made him a tiny curtsey. 'Yes, sir,' she managed. He didn't appreciate it at all. The Mercedes snarled at both of them as it whipped out of the parking lot.

It was not until the battered van was halfway home that the problem suddenly seemed no longer funny. Mrs Corey? Good lord, not married to that—that! Well, not! What would her grandfather have said? He would have pushed her into marriage, that's what! They were both alike, these two men—both pirates of the first water! But this one *loves* his little girl, and that's a word Grandfather would never have admitted.

By the time they reached Navigation Lane Penny Harris was a sobered woman, deep in the entanglements of her past, while Abigail Corey was as cheerful as a girl could be, dreaming happily about her future.

He came back at seven that night, long after the two girls had eaten and cleared away. He walked in without knocking, accepted his daughter's adulation, and hardly paying any attention to the cool looks that Penny was transmitting.

'What, no dinner?' he commented, as he sat down by the clean kitchen table.

'I'm not running an Inn,' Penny snapped at him. 'And I don't remember any arrangements to take in permanent boarders! Don't you think it's about time for you to try living in your own house?'

He looked up at her, startled. 'Why I thought all Cape Codders were hospitable to a fault.' She shook her head. Life had become so confusing that she no longer could tell whether he was for real.

'Maybe they are,' she snapped at him, 'but I'm not a

Cape Codder. I'm a Bostonian, and we're noted for meanness, inhospitality, and reckless driving!'

'I don't believe that either,' he said. 'I've known a great many Bostonians. Man and boy they were fine people, full of welcome to strangers. What have you to say about that?'

'You may not have noticed,' she growled, 'but I am neither man nor boy!'

'I do believe she means it, Abby!'

'I'm sure you can get food in your own house,' Penny snarled. 'I'm not operating a fast-food counter, Mr Corey!'

'You hear that, Abby? She really does mean it.' He moved across the room to his daughter's side. 'We don't have any food in our house,' he sighed, 'and the beds aren't set up either. I can see how you would object to having me around all the time, but surely you don't intend to put Abigail out in the cold, do you?'

Penny shook herself, trying to free her mind from the maze into which he was pushing her. Everything is crazy about this man, she told herself. There's no top nor bottom to his world. He seems to ride around in circles, and he's got *me* going with him! 'No,' she snapped, 'Abby is always welcome in my house!'

'Then it's just me you object to?'

The words crowding into her throat tried to tumble out. None of them made it. Yes, she wanted to shout at him. It's you who's unwelcome in my house. It's you, you arrogant, homely—lovable——! And that was the roadblock. I don't really know *what* I feel about him, she told herself. He's got me too confused to make sense. When he's around I don't *want* to make sense. I just want to—I don't know what I just want to!

'Why don't we step outside and discuss this sensibly,' he said, 'out of the reach of sensitive little pitchers.'

Go outside with you? What kind of a stupid woman do you think I am, she thought. With all that moonlight and starshine I'd be like a sitting duck! And yet some strained female voice was saying, 'Abby, why don't you go up and have a bath while your father and I talk something over. Take a good long soak, and then try out the new pyjamas we bought.'

'Yeah, great—Mommy,' the child sang. She rushed over to Penny and jumped up at her, hanging around her neck with two slender arms until Penny's enveloped her.

'I'm not your mama,' she whispered in the girl's ear. Abby giggled, as she ran for the stairs.

'Well?' He was holding the back door open for her. She snatched up her yellow windbreaker, zipped it full up, and stalked out in front of him.

He's too close, the alarms in the back of her head warned. Bells were ringing, whistles blowing, all in her head. He's too close, they all signalled. She tried to move away from him. He accepted it all as an invitation. His hand folded under the crook of her elbow, and before she could formulate a complaint he was urging her around the house and down the slight incline that brought Navigation Lane flat and even with the tuftings of the saltmarsh.

The tide was coming in, and the moon was bright. Water splashed on all sides of them as the night life of the Marsh went about its business. The world was so quiet that they could hear the putter of a fishing boat, feeling its way back into port, up off Beach Point. The stars blinked at them, distant and cold. She shivered. He put his arm around her, and almost as if it were an old habit, she continued the walk with her head on his shoulder. A hundred feet down the road he stopped them. 'This is far enough,' he said softly.

'What—what did you want to talk about?' she asked, barely able to bring the words out through the aura of comfort that surrounded her.

'Just this,' he replied. He pulled her around to face him, bent the few inches needed, and touched his lips to hers. She felt the gentle warmth of it, the comfort, the peace. But then, instead of freeing her, he pulled her tighter, closer, and increased the pressure of his lips.

It was something she was not prepared for, and yet she knew she had been waiting for this all the days of her life. She moaned, opened her lips to him, and submerged herself in the passion that followed. It seemed to go on for hours, this wild sweet communion that shook her mind to its core. She clung to him, squeezing frantically closer, violently responsive as one of his hands wandered up and down her back, around the narrow bridge of her waist, down to her hips, and back up again. It was a tender movement from which she did not want an escape. He finally ended it, moving away from her lips, dropping a touch of a kiss on her earlobes, and then, almost regretfully, putting a little space between them. Her eyes had closed at the first asssault. Now they opened, as she tried to read his expression in the moonlight. His face was shuttered. She moaned a little objection, and tried to move closer to him, but his arms held tight at her elbows, and would not allow it.

Feelings began to awaken within her. Her toes ached. She had been standing on them, arched upward, all this time, and hadn't realised it. Her hands twitched as she dropped them to her sides. She breathed deeply, refilling long-emptied lungs, and eventually things returned almost to normal.

What an idiot you are, Penny Harris, she lectured herself. It's all moonlight and quiet winds. He's a man, and you're a woman, and what else would you expect? Love? Stupid girl. You've got both feet on the ground now—and a lovely memory. Leave it at that and get on with living.

'What do you think about it all now?' he asked softly.

'Me?' she sighed. 'What would you like for supper?'

CHAPTER FIVE

SHE was surprised how easy it was to slip into a routine totally different from anything she had ever imagined. For the first week she drove Abby to school at eight in the morning and picked her up at three. Thereafter she needed only to drive the child to the head of the lane, where a bus picked her up in the morning and dropped her off in the evening. As for Frank, she hardly knew what to say. He kept repeating that his job on the Cape was finished, yet every morning he came over from the other house, joined them for breakfast, then drove off in his Mercedes. And never a word about where he was going, why he went, or when he might be back.

'And as for me,' Penny teased herself, 'I might just as well be married to him. His daughter lives here. He does too, practically speaking, although he goes next door to sleep nights.' He paid for everything: the food, his daughter's clothes, the utility bills, everything. He even offered her a salary, which she declined with some heat. 'And maybe I ought to have my head examined,' she mumbled. 'Look at me, elbow-deep in dish water, cleaning house, running errands. I ought to charge him twenty dollars an hour, that's what!'

There had been no repetition of that walk down the lane, that had ended in the 'Kiss of Death', as she labelled it. Death to all her plans for the future. 'But I'm not going to let *him* know,' she grumbled as she dried the last of the dishes. 'I don't know why he stays in the lane, if his job is really finished. I don't know where he lives when he's not living here. And I don't even care!' Which was the biggest lie she had ever told herself.

The hardest part of it all had been the long arguments with his daughter. Day after day Abby kept

calling her 'Mother'. And that was out of bounds. At
the end of the first week they managed a compromise.
'Aunt Penny', she was now called, and although it made
her feel like some elderly shrew sitting in a corner, it
was something she could put up with.

With a sigh she pulled the plug in the sink and
watched the water swirl and struggle down the drain.
Her mind automatically made a note. The cesspool
which served all three houses was definitely giving up
the ghost, unable to function against the water-pressure
in the marshes. She gave the empty sink a brisk
scrubbing and started on the rest of the house.

Two hours later, satisfied with her own house, she
decided to give *his* house a quick cleaning. It was a
subject she had debated for days, but could just not
work up the courage. He had left her a front-door key, 'In
case of fire,' he said. So, knowing that he would be away
for the day, and Abby would be at school until three,
she gathered up the tools of her trade and went over.

The house was a duplicate of her own. All three of
the buildings had been constructed to the same set of
blueprints. But no sooner had she fumbled her way in
through the front door than her life puzzle became even
more confused. Crates and boxes filled the living room
and kitchen in exactly the same order they had been left
by the movers. 'Why, that's stupid,' she mumbled
aloud. 'He hasn't unpacked a thing! What kind of a
home is this?'

The further she went the worse it got. Throughout
the entire house the sum total of his *housekeeping*
consisted of setting up a single bed and mattress
upstairs in the bedroom that corresponded with her
own. No sheets, no blankets, just the bed, the mattress,
and a sleeping bag sprawled across the top. She went
downstairs again very slowly, and out into the October
sun to think things over.

The questions weren't new. It was just that there
weren't any answers. For thirty days they had lived in
each other's pocket, and he was still a gypsy, not even

bothering to unpack what he had newly purchased for his 'home'. What does he do for a living? Where does he do it? Why do I get the idea that at any moment he's going to get in his car and drive off? And what will he leave behind if he does? Me? Abby? A houseful of furniture he doesn't want? What the devil good has all my protest done for me?

She grumbled her way back to her own house, pacing along slowly, her tall neat figure slumping badly, her hands twisting together behind her back. A flashback from the television re-runs of her youth, the ancient black-and-white programmes, and it was just enough to pull her out of the doldrums. 'Who is that Masked Man, anyway?' she smiled. And that's the way he found her as he rattled up into her driveway with something different, a four-wheel drive Jeep.

She had intended to ask him something important the first time she saw him today. It all flew out the window. Instead she managed to squeeze out, 'New car?'

'Hardly,' he replied grimly as he stalked her. She could see the storm lines in his face, and backed away from him until the front doorknob dug into her hip.

'I've got to talk to you,' he growled. She tried to squirm back a little further, to no good result. 'You don't have to run away,' he added as he watched her try to dive into the woodwork. 'I won't eat you.'

'Oh,' she sputtered. 'You've *had* your lunch?'

He shook his head slowly. 'How can a lovely, intelligent woman talk so stupidly?' he asked.

'It's easy.' Her throat was drying up, making conversation difficult—more difficult than it had been. 'I practise a lot.' She squeaked in alarm as both of his hands landed flat against the door, one on either side of her. 'And it doesn't help when you try to scare me,' she snapped. Injured innocence, that's the trick, she told herself. He scares me! Well, he doesn't, but it might be a good excuse. It's not scaring that he's doing, it's—I don't know what it is, do I?

'Me scare a great big girl like you?' he chuckled. 'I'm

only a couple of inches taller than you, and I haven't studied karate. I'm the one who's being threatened!'

'Yeah, sure,' she snarled. 'And you'd better look out! I'm pretty mean when I have to be! Why are you trapping me here?'

He looked down at his hands as if surprised to see them blocking her way. 'I don't honestly know,' he said. 'Do you?'

'No, I don't know,' she sighed as her arms slipped around his neck and pulled his head down those vital two inches. His lips were soft on hers, soft and enticing, daring her. Her experience failed her again. Having taken the first step, she had no idea what came next. 'Like this,' he murmured in her ear.

His lips touch-typed their way across the lobe of her ear, the soft pulse on her neck, and then back to her lips. Her half-opened mouth, almost prepared to question, proved an easy target for his assault. All the warmth in the world crowded in on her as his tongue provoked, and his wandering hands explored. For one small second she rebelled, trying to force him off. It was a futile gesture. It's hard to fight off a man when both your own hands insist on remaining wrapped together at the nape of his neck. Her token resistance flared and disappeared, to be replaced by wild sensation as one of his hands slipped through the opening in her jacket and settled on the seething mound of her breast. 'Don't,' she gasped.

'Don't what?' he demanded.

'I don't know,' she whispered. The hand found the buttons of her blouse, and its warmth slipped inside, under her camisole top. She gasped at the shock. The bronze tip, under his questing fingers, snapped to attention. Her blood pumped harder, her nerves jumped under the scalding attack as he drew back from her lips to breathe. That one sweet pause restored her control, just as if someone had thrown a pail of water at her.

'No,' she said more firmly. Her hands came down, a little late, to defend herself. He resisted for a moment, and then slowly withdrew that buccaneer hand. His eyes, only inches from hers, bored holes in her.

'No?' he asked patiently.

'No!' Her reply was firm, flat, positive.

'Nice girls don't do that sort of thing?'

'That's right,' she managed. He nodded his head and stepped back from her. 'No, of course they don't,' he muttered, half under his breath. 'What *do* they do?'

'I don't know,' she said, 'but they don't do that! Did you rush back here just to seduce me?'

'Hardly,' he grinned. 'If I had it would be all over by now.'

'It *is* over by now,' she said primly. 'Think of yourself as highly experienced with women, do you?'

'I *do* have that reputation,' he returned. 'Or at least I've been told by various members of your sex that that's true. But you're unattainable, right? Virtue protects you, and all that?'

'Probably,' she sighed again. 'At least it does before lunch, after I've spent a couple of hours house-cleaning. It's true, isn't it? Men think about sex morning, noon and night? That's all that's on your minds!'

It seemed she had stuck a pin in him. 'Lord no,' he retorted, turning back towards the Jeep. 'There's something I want to show you, but not here. This isn't the right place for it. Hop in.'

He held the door open. She managed the high entry with no trouble at all, her long legs clearing the sill with a grace he stopped to admire.

'Why not here?' she asked anxiously.

'Because you've acquired another watcher,' he said. She looked over at him. He was pursing his lips in and out, in and out. It was a sign she had learned to read. He was thinking of something, and he was not likely to tell her about it until he was ready. Which irritated her more than she would like to admit.

'Is he still over at Sandy Neck?'

'No, up the lane. He's watching the junction at Route 6A.'

'So isn't it pretty—stupid—for us to drive right by him?'

'I think not,' he barked at her. 'I think he'll watch us go right by him, and then he'll come down and search the house.'

'But he can't do that,' she yelled at him above the noise of the engine. Invasion of privacy, she told herself. It rattled her mind to think of some stranger pawing through her things, prying in her corners, poking his nose into her life. 'We'll come back behind him and beat up on him,' she suggested hopefully.

'Maybe,' he grunted. 'Watch for the green Subaru on the right. Regular little firebrand, aren't you!' He didn't seem too displeased about the idea.

'I'm *not* little,' she snapped at him, and squared away in her seat.

'Dead ahead of us,' he commented. 'He's watching. Making sure we're both accounted for, I guess.'

'So why are you going so slowly?'

'I want to see—ah, there he goes. A U-turn and down the lane he goes.'

'He can't do that,' she sniffed. 'U-turns are illegal in Barnstable County.'

'So he'll worry,' he chuckled. 'Hey, lady, this guy might be out for blood, and all you're worried about is making a U-turn?'

'I'm not worried *just* about U-turns,' she snapped. 'I seem to be worried about everything in the world. Would you believe it, until I was fourteen they used to call me Hap?'

'Hap?'

'A nickname—for Happy. I was always singing and dancing around, and laughing. God, I wish I could have a good laugh. I wish—why is the world so darn miserable?'

'Only on special days. Come on now, little—I mean—lady. The first thing you know somebody is going to start calling you Mercury.'

'That doesn't make sense.'

'Because you keep zooming up and down daily like

the mercury in a thermometer,' he explained. It wasn't worth an answer. She composed herself, sat up stiffly in her seat, crossed her arms over her breasts, and watched the roadside whistle by. He continued on Route 6A until they passed over Scorton creek, and then turned right, on to the Sandy Neck road. As they came closer to the shore of Massachusetts Bay she could smell the salt air and hear the booming of the breakers. He stopped at the end of the road. 'We walk from here,' he said.

She looked down her nose at him and climbed out of the vehicle with as much regal posturing as she could muster. He knew what she was up to. 'After you, princess.' He offered a bow and a broad sweeping gesture down the beach. She sniffed. It was the only thing that came to mind. He slipped off his boots and went ploughing eastward through the fine-grained sand. There was hardly anything else to do; she stripped off her sandals and followed.

Although her legs were long, her breath was short. 'Do we have to set a new track record?' she managed to squeak.

'No,' he called, stopping to wait for her. 'Force of habit.'

'Are we going around to where that other detective was watching our houses?'

'Not right this minute. This is far enough.' He had found a perfectly clear patch of sand above the high water mark, and dropped down on it. She stood above him and looked down, hands thrust into the pockets of her jacket. The off-shore wind was chilling, whistling in her ear and filling her nostrils with that good salt air. The sun had warmed some parts of the beach. 'Why here?' she asked.

'Why not?' he returned. 'It's nice here. I like the view over the water, I like to watch the boats. For God's sake sit down. Don't make an issue of every single thing that comes up.'

'You don't have to be nasty about it,' she complained.

'You've met a lot of nicer men than me?'

She nodded her head. 'And better looking, too.'

'That wouldn't be hard to do,' he said. 'Sit down. You keep complaining about people towering over you, but you do it yourself every chance you get.' He patted the sand beside him, and that lopsided grin spread. Damn it, she muttered to herself, who said a leopard can't change its spots? He does it all the time. He's a chameleon—a great big overgrown chameleon.

'Stop talking to yourself and read this.' He thrust a copy of the *Boston Globe* in front of her. A felt pen had isolated one story. She took the paper, turned her back to the sun, and started to read. The smile which had sneaked up on her while he was talking slowly faded away. It was a short story, a filler in the business section. 'Fund Directors Vote to Dissolve', the little headline read. The story was equally brief. The board of directors of the Philip Harris Foundation, at their meeting in October, had voted to dissolve the Foundation and disperse all the money remaining in the treasury. Because of legal restriction, another affirmative vote would be required in November to complete the action.

She sat there holding the paper in front of her long after she had finished reading it. Dissolve the fund? And in November, two months before she could legally take over the direction for herself? Two months.

It wasn't that *she* wanted the money. Her year of independence had shown her that she could make a living for herself. It did have something to do with Uncle Henry, who did not deserve a penny. Nor his long list of relatives! But mostly it had to do with Grandfather, the solemn stern man who had raised her according to his best beliefs, and wanted something specific done with his money. And only she knew what that was.

'They've beaten me, haven't they?' she said softly. He moved a little closer and put one strong hand over hers.

'Perhaps,' he said. 'But it's not over until November the fifteenth. Do you really want the money that badly?'

'I *don't* want the money,' she told him. 'I want control of the money. There's something I have to do.' She was looking out on to the bay when she said it, and missed the flash of pain that swept across his face.

'In that case,' he said grimly, 'you need a smart lawyer.'

'You?' she asked eagerly.

'Not me. I said you needed a *smart* lawyer. Not me.'

'But I'd feel a great deal better if it were you.'

'No chance, lady. A lawyer who's emotionally involved in a case can never be objective in court. He'd miss something. I'd rather see you uncomfortable before the crisis than after.' He turned his back on her and began scaling pebbles into the water.

A lawyer who's emotionally involved? she thought. What does *that* mean? That's he's—no, not with me. Things still haven't changed. I'm the girl where he's at, so I can expect these passes, but nothing more. If he really felt something for me, he'd say so. What can he—of course! Aunt Penny. His *daughter* is emotionally involved, and he's looking after *her* interests all the time. There are some times, she told herself fiercely, that I wish I'd never set eyes on that little girl. Or her father! Why me? Didn't I have enough troubles before that for any one woman?

'Will you recommend a lawyer for me?' she asked quietly. Don't let emotion show in your voice. Don't look at him. Don't—don't do anything.

'No, I won't recommend a lawyer. I'll *get* you one. The best in the Commonwealth. It'll take a couple of days.'

'But I don't have a couple of days to spare, do I?'

'Well, we'll see. There aren't any guarantees in law.' He folded up his knees, clasped his arms around them, and seemed to be following the flight of a couple of gulls who were diving about a hundred yards off shore.

'I really can't afford the best,' she reminded him. 'I

just don't have the money.' He waved her objection aside.

'If he wins, you'll have plenty of money,' he said. 'If he doesn't win, then he doesn't deserve to get paid.'

And that seemed to end *that* conversation. They sat side by side for another five minutes. The sun ducked behind a high cumulus cloud, and suddenly the beach really felt like October. She zipped up her jacket. 'Don't you think we could go back now?'

He consulted his watch. 'Not yet. That guy needs another half hour or so. I want him to find the stuff I planted in your house. It will perhaps give us a few more days' respite.'

'You planted something in my house?'

'Yes.' He got to his feet and extended a hand. 'I wanted to give him something to think about.' She took the hand, and he pulled her easily to her feet. 'We'd better walk down the beach. It's too cold just to sit.' She started after him, but he stopped and took her arm. It improved her walking ability by almost a hundred percent, she noticed. Everything is so much easier when you're having fun!

'What was it you planted?' They had gone another few hundred feet down the beach, and he was turning up towards the crest of the dunes. For the first time she noticed the binocular case at his side.

'A gun,' he reported, 'and a police badge. If he's any good he's bound to find them!'

'A gun in my house! Why—Frank Corey, you have a nerve! I don't like guns. What if Abby—when did you plant them? Where?'

'Last night, in the drawer where you keep your knives and forks.'

'Well, I've never heard such a thing,' she gasped at him. Climbing up the dune, two steps up, one back, was wearing her out. 'What if Abby poked around and found them? They do, you know—poke around. All kids do. She could have been hurt!'

'So all of a sudden you're a child expert?' She was

happy to hear that he was short of breath, too. They had reached the summit. 'We can't stop here on the skyline.' His hand urged her down the other side, until they were below the level of the crest. 'Now, you were saying about what all kids do?'

She plumped herself down, all out of wind. He stood over her. Towered over her. I'm going to get some shoes with *four*-inch heels, she promised herself grimly. 'Well?' he prompted. He's laughing at me, she told herself. Damn the man. Just as soon as I get some breath I'm going to——

'He's leaving already,' he interrupted. The binoculars were clamped to his eyes, scanning the scene across the harbour from them. 'Going like a bat out of hell. He's either found the bait, or been bitten by rattlesnakes.'

'They don't have rattlesnakes out here,' she told him primly. He was following the movement of the car screaming up Navigation Lane. Even with her naked eye she could see the plume of dust. He stood there with glasses locked on target. And that's something else he can do that I can't, she told herself. He does a lot of things better than I do. She shrugged her shoulders, discouraged. For just once she would like to be able to show him something. Just once!

'About the kids?' he prodded.

'I read it in a book,' she mumbled. 'Can we go back now? I have to have lunch.'

'Can't miss a meal?' he enquired.

'No, I can't,' she snarled at him. 'Sometimes I think you're a very uncouth person, Mr Corey. Sometimes I don't understand how such a nice little girl like Abby could really be your daughter!'

'You're not alone in that,' he said. 'Wait until you see the rest of my family. Come on, I'm eager to see that he found everything!' She struggled to her feet. He moved towards her, reaching for her arm. She backed away. His laughter defused her anger, but she still felt the need to punish him somehow. As if not touching her would punish him! Hah!

He started to say something, saw the glint in her eyes, and refused to join battle. She ploughed up the sand dune a few steps behind him, and down the other side. He strolled up the beach, hands in his pockets, whistling. She kept her distance, but gradually the laughter surfaced. He was a terrible whistler.

They were back at the house in thirty minutes. Despite his statement about haste, he drove slowly. She kept her eyes straight ahead and sat on the outer edge of her seat. The highway traffic was heavy at the noon hour, and it became a challenge to make a left turn off Route 6A. As soon as the car cleared the crossing however, he pulled to a stop in the middle of the lane, set the handbrake, and turned to look at her. His grin seemed wider than his face.

'You're a terrible whistler,' she giggled.

'No, you've got it wrong. I'm a good whistler, but I'm tone deaf!'

'Well, thank God for that,' she said with an exaggerated sigh. 'And here all the time I was trying to adjust to the idea that you were the perfect man!'

He sat for a moment, staring. Then his bass laughter joined her contralto giggles. She slid over in the seat within companionable distance. His hand stretched the rest of the way, covering both of hers, where they rested in her lap.

'Well thank God for *that*!' He copied her words and intonations. 'I would hate to have lunch under the Rule of Silence! You're a nice lady, Penny Bloom? Penny Harris?

'Penny Bloom Harris,' she returned solemnly. 'You're a nice man, Frank Corey.'

'Even if I'm not handsome?'

'Did I say that?' Her hand went up to his cheek and traced a small circle on it. 'You have to shave twice a day, I'll bet.'

'It depends entirely on what I'm doing at night,' he said. And you're playing a dangerous game, Penny Harris, her conscience noted loudly. Hush! Anything you say from here on in, he'll think of as an invitation, and you're not ready for that, either. Are you? Neither he nor her conscience received an answer. She locked her lips and shut off her mind, and just enjoyed the world as he started the Jeep and went down towards the house.

'Don't touch anything,' he told her as he led the way into the house.

'It doesn't look as if anyone's been here,' she whispered. 'Why am I whispering? He's gone, hasn't he?' A delicious shiver ran up and down her spine. A little adventure, that's what I need, she told herself. A little rough and tumble adventure. What's he doing with that magnifying glass? Good Lord, Sherlock Holmes? So ask! She did.

'Here,' he informed her, 'I glued a couple of hairs across the drawer. They've been broken. So he looked in here.'

'So?'

'So that's where the gun and the badge are. Watch this.' He pulled the unit out gently. Among the stainless steel utensils she could see the gun and the badge, nestling close to each other. 'He's not as good as I thought,' Frank laughed. 'I had the badge on the *other* side of the gun. Which means he took the thing out and looked at it. And if he concludes what I think he will, your Uncle Henry will get the message some time today that there's a police sergeant assigned to guard you, night and day. And that ought to make him think a time or two!'

'Why, Frank,' she laughed, 'you're not only a nice man, you're devious too!'

'I admit it,' he returned. 'Now why don't you thank me properly?'

'I—properly? I——'

'Like this.' He swept her up against himself, his head bent over, shutting out the sunlight, and his lips sealed hers. He had caught her unawares again, but this time she had no desire to struggle. She went softly and cooperatively into the strong shelter he offered, and surrendered herself to the feelings that ran riot up and down her frame. His tongue played havoc with her tender mouth, and then he shifted to her throat, her earlobes, and lower.

With her eyes glued shut she clung to him, hardly noticing as his hand ripped down the zipper of her jacket and slipped it off her shoulders. He bent and his kisses went lower, to the point where her buttoned blouse shut off access to his target. Her head was swirling, running riot, as his warm fingers did away with the obstructions. Her blouse followed her jacket to the floor. The straps of her camisole top followed down her arms. She gasped in surprised delight as his hands and then his mouth cherished her firm full breasts. She lay back against the curve of his arm, eyes still closed, hands running through his hair as he devoured her. He had changed. No longer the laughing companion, he was the hunter on the trail. The insistent thought projected into her brain, below the level of the sensation he was causing. He stopped.

'Hell,' he groaned, 'what are we doing standing here when there's a great empty bed upstairs?' He didn't wait for an answer. His right arm swept under her knees as he picked her up off the floor and started for the stairs. She opened her eyes, fear hiding just beneath their lids. He seemed totally entranced by her swaying breasts, and the sublimated message in her mind managed to rise to the surface. As his foot reached for the first tread of the stairs she grabbed at the banister.

'No, Frank,' she moaned. 'No!'

'No?' He seemed to doubt his own ears.

'Yes,' she sighed, 'I mean no, Frank.'

'You want it as much as I do,' he said grimly. 'This is no time to stop the train, lady.'

'I think I want it *more* than you do,' she moaned, 'but I can't. I never have. I never will, not this way. I haven't much in this world except myself, and I mean to save that for—for a wedding gift to the right man—

when he comes along.' She watched his eyes, flashing a pleading signal that he could not ignore. His arms were shaking, agitating her breasts, causing him to shake even more. He was walking a tightrope that might lead them both to disaster. And then she saw him clamp his muscles, firm his mouth, and set her down. She backed away from him, up against the wall, and frantically struggled to pull up the straps of her camisole.

'No,' he grated. One of his fingers extended and touched the tips of her breasts, then he slid the straps back in place himself.

'No,' he repeated, in a voice cold as ice. He stared at her blushing face, her quivering shoulders which had not yet been released from the emotional tension of his hands. His tongue came out and wetted his dry lips. He pushed by her and sauntered up the stairs. She shuddered, and went back to the kitchen. She could hear the shower running upstairs. Despite being all thumbs, she managed to get herself back into her blouse and hang up her jacket.

And what do I do next? she asked herself. If I were sophisticated I suppose I could laugh it off. But I'm not. So? Make lunch. Put your fingers to work. Do something now. Settle down before he comes back again, and put it all out of your mind. *If you can*, her conscience niggled at her. *If you can. Pandora couldn't close the lid again, could she?*

In another twenty minutes he came back downstairs, as neat as a pin, his face arranged in its worst possible state. 'Lunch,' she offered hesitantly.

'Lunch,' he agreed. They both sat down at the table. She served the chicken noodle soup in a pair of chowder dishes, being careful to keep the cracked one for herself. 'Nice soup,' he commented as he spooned up the last drop. 'I thought you only cooked eggs?'

'I'm very handy with a can opener too,' she whispered. 'Did you want coffee with your sandwiches?' He nodded an affirmative. The kettle was whistling. She fumbled instant coffee into the mugs and took them to the table. He was already attacking the sandwiches.

'I hope—I—are the sandwiches okay?'

'Marvellous,' he said. He leaned over the table and fingered her chin. 'I'm not angry with you,' he sighed. 'You have the absolute right to do whatever you want with your own body.'

There was a small tear in her eye. He brushed it away with his thick finger, and went back to his sandwiches.

'I'll pick Abby up this afternoon,' he said as she got up to clear the table. 'I have to make some long-distance calls, and it would be better if I go over to the telephone centre. Those were unusual sandwiches, Penny.' She looked down at her plate, where her own rested, untouched.

She hated to ask, but could not stop herself. 'Unusual?'

'Yes,' he said. 'I thought it was interesting to have peanut butter on the tuna fish sandwich, but the jelly on the toasted cheese was an absolute stroke of genius!'

He went out the door whistling. She heard the tyres squeal as he drove away. She sat at the table and stared at the sandwiches, not really seeing them. Her right hand absentmindedly went up to finger her own breast as she tried to come to terms with her mad sexuality. The memories returned. They followed her all afternoon.

CHAPTER SIX

'OH my, that won't do,' Abby said as Penny came downstairs still rubbing the sleep from her eyes.

'What won't do?' Penny returned as she glanced up at the wall clock. 'Good heavens, girl, it's almost nine o'clock. You're late for school! How in the world did I oversleep so badly? That darn alarm clock! I must have forgotten to set it!'

'You didn't,' the child giggled. 'Daddy came over early and shut off your alarm 'cause he said you had a hard day yesterday, and it was gonna be worse today so you needed all the sleep you could get and I don't have to go to school 'cause I'm gonna go with you. And you gotta wear a dress!'

'Well,' Penny laughed, 'that was more than a mouthful.' Don't they teach you about periods in your school? Short sentences? Things like that?' And then as an afterthought, 'Why do I need to wear a dress to go wherever it is we're going to go?'

'Daddy didn't tell you?'

'Tell me what?' Penny had only a portion of her mind on the conversation. A pot of real perked coffee was steaming by the kitchen sink. Real coffee, and she was dying for her usual two or three cups before the world was turned on. She shuffled over and poured herself a mug, sipping gratefully, and giving thanks to whatever cat burglar it was who had broken in to provide such delightful service. 'Nice,' she murmured.

'You should've tasted the pancakes he made for me,' Abby answered. 'He can do 'most anything, my dad can.'

'Your dad made all this? Where did I get the idea that he wouldn't know a kitchen from a garbage scow? And where is he?'

'He went to that place. I forget the name. To make sure they got here, and were ready to meet you. And that's why you gotta wear a dress. You gotta meet your lawyer. That's what my dad said. And if you don't wear a dress she'll be mad, 'cause women are supposed to wear dresses. Me, too. I gotta wear a dress, or she'll murder me!'

Penny sipped at the blessed coffee and smiled at the child. 'She? My lawyer is a woman?'

'No,' Abby giggled. 'He's a man. He likes girls to wear dresses too, but when Daddy called him she said she was coming too, and there ain't nobody says no to Grandma.'

'Isn't,' Penny corrected automatically. 'Not ain't— isn't. I'm not sure what the devil you're talking about, but if it's that important we'd better get bustling. Grandma, huh? It'll be a nice day for you to wear your dirndl skirt, and that white blouse with the penguins on it. As soon as you clean your plate, upstairs and wash, young lady. You've got maple syrup all over your chin!'

And while you do that, she thought to herself, I'll try to open my other eye and find out what's going on in this crazy world. Nine o'clock, would you believe that? So I had a hard day yesterday? I'm glad he realises it. And today can't possibly be as hard. I won't let him come within ten yards of me if I can help it!

She reached for the coffee-pot and refilled her mug. Half-way through the new dosage she heard the Mercedes scream into the driveway. A quick look into the kitchen mirror spoiled her morning.

'So here I am, the sophisticated Penelope Harris,' she muttered. 'Hair like a rat's nest, a nightgown that's too small and too old, a robe the Salvation Army wouldn't accept, and not a bit of make-up. Look at that horror!'

She could hear his footsteps at the front door. Abandoning the coffee mug she raced for the stairs. She was half-way up when the front door opened, and she simultaneously tripped over the hem of her robe. There were two thumps. One was the front door closing, the other marked the sudden halt as her well-rounded bottom lit on the stair. She squirmed around, facing down the stairs, losing the tie on her robe and one of her slippers as well.

'Now that's real art,' he called from the bottom of the stairs.

'What the devil are you babbling about?' she snarled. She stood up slowly, gently rubbing her injured fundament.

'That.' He waved at her frontage. She glanced down. The robe was hanging open, her nightgown was hitched up above her knees, and her breasts were distorting the semi-transparent cotton of her bodice.

'Damn!' she muttered, grabbing the lapels of the robe. 'You——'

'Me?' he asked in all innocence. 'What did I have to do with anything?'

'This sort of thing never happened to me before I met you,' she accused. He put one foot on the stairs. She backed up, not daring to turn her back on him, still clutching madly at her robe. He took two more quick steps. She turned and fled.

'Twenty minutes,' he called after her. 'That's all the time we have to spare.'

She stumbled into her room, muttering a few of the words she had once heard her grandfather say. 'Damn!' she muttered. The mirror on the back of her door reflected too much truth. She stomped around the room in circles until her anger had dissipated. It was *all* his fault. Everything! If he had never moved into the Lane, things would still be—damn! Five minutes had elapsed. And I certainly am not going to let him tie me to a clock, she told herself. But she did hurry, and found herself with two minutes to spare. She used them for tearing that nightgown into strips, and jamming them into the waste basket. The exercise did a great deal for her state of mind.

Both Abby and Frank were waiting for her when she came down. The little girl looked the picture of charm, except that her hair had no rhyme or reason to it. 'Daddy did that for me,' she piped up. 'Wasn't that nice of him?'

'Very nice,' Penny said non-committally. 'We'll just touch it up a little while he's driving us—to where we're going.' She glared at him. 'And wouldn't it be nice if someone would explain to me just what's going on?' He faked a little shiver, and turned up the collar of his suit coat, as if a sudden cold wave had just blown in.

And how very nice *he* looks, she told herself. A three-piece grey suit, some sort of old school tie, shoes glistening, hair brushed smartly. Altogether tasty. The thought brought a blush. She turned her back on him, trying to hide the tell-tale signs.

She was wearing a suit herself. A navy-blue pleated skirt, a golden blazer, and under it a demurely conservative blouse that buttoned to the throat, with a frill of lace. My *go to see the lawyer* suit, she had told herself upstairs, but now she wasn't so sure. Too conservative? But it followed her form in all the right places. And for some reason she wanted that today.

'Let's go,' he interrupted.

'Go where?' she snapped.

'Sandwich. The oldest town on the Cape. 1637.' She sniffed, and ran her fingers through Abby's hair. 'I don't need a guide book,' she said softly so only he could hear. 'Maybe not long enough to repair the damage to Abby's hair!'

'Smart Alec,' he returned, equally softly. She wore a tight smile as she followed him out to the Mercedes. Maybe that second word had had only *one* syllable. She pulled her shoulders back, straightened her blazer, and glared at the back of his neck. The pose was too hard to hold. By the time the car began to move she was back to her sunniest disposition, and her busy hands were re-arranging Abby's hairdo.

It's a very short drive from Navigation Lane to the bypass that leads down into the centre of old Sandwich village. They drove past the entrance to the State

Forest, where pine trees towered a hundred feet into the air. The road changed from Route 6A to Main Street, and wandered between small cottages, and larger homes set back from the street. Some were new; others dated back as far as 1650. They presented a common front. Practically all of them sported a 'bed and breakfast' sign.

In the very centre of the village stood the First Church of Christ, a white wooden church with a soaring spire that screamed of Christopher Wren design. And down the street, on the other side of the Green, was the Dan'l Webster Inn.

The central part of the Inn was a square wooden structure in Colonial Federal style, red painted, with two long and much more modern wings. Frank drove them up under the front portico and helped them both out. 'Look at that,' Abby shrilled. 'A real sleigh, but no horses!' She sounded very disappointed.

'It's only October,' her father reminded her. 'Why would they put the horses to a sleigh this early?'

'Daddy, you don't have any imagination,' the child teased.

'And you'd better behave yourself,' he chuckled as he demonstrated the old-fashioned set of stocks that stood to one side of the sleigh. 'Come on now, we've wasted enough time. I suspect everyone is waiting for us.

'You still haven't told me who we're going to meet,' Penny insisted as he took her by the elbow and hurried her into the lobby.

'Don't drag your feet,' he snapped. 'You'll see soon enough.' He walked her through the length of the building and out to the glass-walled conservatory, in the very rear. A cluster of tables had been set together, with five people seated around it. Penny stared, suddenly shy. Abby settled her problem for her. She seized Penny's hand and towed her round the circle to where the only woman sat, a white-haired and rather plump lady to whom the years had been kind. She seemed to perch on her chair like a tiny Pouter Pigeon,

completely surrounded by the four huge men who
shared the table. Surrounded, but never overwhelmed.

'Grandma!' the child said excitedly. 'This is Penny.
Ain't she pretty?'

'So,' the little lady said, 'this is Penny. We've heard
so much about you, my dear.' She pushed her chair
back from the table and stood up, barely five foot three
tall. Penny could feel that nervousness that always
affected her in the presence of authority, but there was
no need. This particular authority came over and threw
her arms around her. It was a warm comforting feeling.
Without knowing exactly why, Penny leaned over and
kissed the soft cheek. The voice that haunted her mind,
that internal conscience of hers, whispered, 'This is
what it feels like to have a mother!' Penny stood there,
flatfooted, unable to muster a word.

'There now,' the older woman said, 'I do believe I'm
going to cry. Somebody bring Penny a chair so she can
sit next to me.' All four of the men rose to comply, but
Frank was ahead of them. 'See,' he whispered in her ear
as he seated her, 'you're a winner already.'

'Maybe,' she returned, 'but what have I won—and
what's the name of the game?'

'Wait and find out,' he whispered, and then sought a
chair for himself, on the far side of the table. Abby had
already settled herself on the other side of her
grandmother and was talking up a storm. The tall,
white-haired man on Penny's right offered a big smooth
hand. 'Michael Corey,' he said. 'For my sins I'm the
father of all these people, and Edith is my wife. You
certainly are a great deal of girl, aren't you? All the rest
of these sons of mine have married little people—as I
did. Nice girls, you understand, but it takes a lot of
bending over to get through a family evening.'

He continued talking casually, but it all went clear
over Penny's head. She was stuck way back in the
conversation with the phrase, 'All the *rest* of them
married little people!' Now what in the world could that
mean? What is it that they all know about me? What

the devil had Frank been telling them? A metallic tapping broke in on her musings. She looked up to find them all staring at her. Frank was tapping his spoon on a plate.

'Penny tends to drift with the tide,' he said. 'Mother asked if you want a second breakfast, and I told her you were still a growing girl and could always eat another meal. And you said?'

'Yes, of course,' she said, blushing stupidly at them all. Frank looked over his shoulder at the waiter. 'We'll both have ham and eggs and coffee,' he said. 'The little girl has had enough food, I think, but I'm sure she could stand a dish of ice cream.'

'Oh yes, I could, Daddy,' Abby said. Me too, Daddy, Penny thought to herself, but I'm a big girl, and I could possibly order for myself, Mr High-Handed-Harry! Mrs Corey leaned forward slightly and stared at her, then smiled.

'You've got it quite wrong,' she said. 'That one over there is my son Harry. Next to him is George. And then my son-in-law Bill. The one you brought in with you is my baby, Frank!'

'So now you've met your match,' Frank laughed. 'I never did get around to telling you that my mother reads minds, did I?'

'It isn't true, is it?' Penny looked at his mother, praying for a negative answer, but the older woman was smiling and nodding. And that ought to teach you something, Penelope Harris, she thought. Now they've even got someone who can read your thoughts! Button up!

'And she blushes,' the tall man to her right laughed. 'Now that's something that's gone out of style!' One of his hands patted her on the head. But look at him. Grandly royal. Tall, with curling white hair, a distinguished and gentlemanly look, and with all that— as handsome as—as his son George and his son Harry, and even his son-in-law Bill. Whatever the devil happened to Frank? And keep your back turned to his mother. She can't possibly read the back of your neck!

She glared across the table at Frank, trying to work up enough anger to really blast him. He was keeping a straight face, but underneath it all she knew he was laughing at her. And suddenly the waiter was there, and the smell of food tempted her. She reached for a fork, managed one mouthful, when Mrs Corey tapped on her arm.

'You must tell me something about your family,' she said. Penny swallowed hard and tried to think of a good answer. There was none, but everyone at the table was looking at her expectantly.

'I—really don't have a family,' she stammered. 'Well, there's my Uncle Henry. He's not exactly my uncle, but I call him that. And—and that's all I have.'

'Why you poor child. Mother? Father?'

'Both dead,' she sighed. 'I never ever knew either of them. My grandfather raised me until I was fourteen and then—Uncle Henry came.'

'That was kind of him, to come and take charge of an adolescent girl?'

'Do you think so—really?'

'He must have loved you, to make such a sacrifice.'

'I don't know,' Penny said. 'If he loved me, he never ever said so. There was a great deal of money, you see.' Just talking about it made Penny shiver. Mrs Corey was studying her face and could see the apprehension. 'I don't think Uncle Henry loved anything except the money,' Penny sighed. 'But perhaps I'm wrong. I was only a kid.'

'Why you poor, poor child! Does it bother you that Frank has stuck his nose in your business?'

'I—no, not really. He's been—very good to me, and I appreciate everything he's tried to do—but he's a hard man to understand.'

'Your Uncle Henry?'

'No, Frank. I—he doesn't even look like his brothers, does he!'

'Ah! My ugly duckling, Frank is now. But—before— he was the most handsome of them all. The last of my boys, you know, and sharper than all of them put together. Even his father has to stand back when Frank goes into action. But handsome? Not any more. Still, I've told him sometime, some place, some lovely girl will have him for what he is, not how he looks. Eat your breakfast, child, while I fend off the little champion chatterer.'

Penny took advantage. She had never expected to get off the hook so quickly. The men were carrying on a separate conversation. Frank's father was scribbling notes in a little blue notebook. One of his brothers was talking into a minirecorder, the other was listening intently, nodding his head. Most of the words had apparently been said; there were only expressions on their faces left to be studied. She did, and learned nothing. Frank smiled at her.

His mother tugged at her sleeve and leaned over towards her. 'See,' she said softly. 'When he smiles he changes, doesn't he? And he seems to smile a great deal at you!'

'He thinks I'm an idiot,' she returned. 'Abby and I get along wonderfully well, but Frank—he either barks at me, scares me, or——'

'Or what?' His mother was all laughter, her face lit up with the joy of living.

'I—nothing,' Penny sighed.

'Eat your breakfast, child.' She picked up her fork and tried to do just that.

'Ain't Penny beautiful?' Abby commented, loudly enough to be heard all around the table. 'And nice, too. That's the kind of mother I'd like to have.'

'Hush, sweetheart,' her grandmother told her. 'You embarrass people when you say things like that.'

'But you always told me to be honest!' There was defiance in the little girl's eyes. 'You told me!'

'You can be honest and quiet at the same time,' her grandmother said pointedly. 'And Penny is indeed a beautiful woman.' Penny's fork, which had been frozen halfway to her mouth when Abby upset the applecart, tried to renew the journey.

'Young lady,' Frank's father said, 'give me a dollar.'

Penny whirled around, dislodging all the egg on her fork, and stared at him with wide eyes. 'Give you a—what?'

'Give me a dollar, young lady. You do have a dollar, don't you?'

'For God's sakes,' Frank threw in, 'she's got forty million of them.' His tone was grim, as it always seemed to be when he mentioned her money. Penny felt the hurt of it, and would not let him get off scot-free this time. She reached down to the floor beside her chair and retrieved her purse. Her plate was still full of breakfast, and she was still hungry, and the eggs were getting cold. Frank's plate was empty, which only added to her anger. She pushed the offending plate aside and upended her purse on the table. Everything fell out. Her comb, two empty lipsticks, one compact, six keys to things she had long forgotten, a wad of tissue, four pencils, all broken, her wristwatch, and a handful of coins.

She pushed everything else aside and concentrated on the coins, counting them aloud as she pushed them to one side. 'And there,' she snapped at Frank, 'is my total wealth. Everything I own. One dollar and eighty-five cents.' Frank flinched as if he expected her to throw some of it at him. His father reached over and appropriated the four quarters.

'From this moment, young lady,' he said, 'I am your lawyer. The dollar is a retainer which you have willingly paid me to represent you. Isn't that true?'

'You're a lawyer, too?' she gasped. 'A dollar isn't much to hire a lawyer with!'

'Yes, I'm a lawyer too,' he laughed, 'and the size of my retainer is not at all to be considered the measure of my ability. We're all lawyers, except for Bill. He's a private detective. Frank is not included in the deal. He is unable to be objective about it. You do want to hire me?'

'I—I certainly need a lawyer,' she gasped, 'but I didn't expect to do it at the breakfast table!'

'Put the rest of your fortune away,' he chuckled. 'We'll get to work on the preliminaries immediately.'

It all sounded so comforting, but so—unexpected that she needed advice. 'Frank?' The question and all its implications were in her voice.

'Yes, Penny,' he returned. 'He's the best lawyer in the state. Something of a shark, very expensive, but the best. These others are just like me—foot soldiers.'

'And you think I should——'

'Yes, I think you should.'

It was all she needed, and it made her angry to admit it—even to herself. One month, and she had quietly, without even realising it, been sliding down the hill into the shadow of Frank Corey. No matter how despicable he was at times, she *depended* on him. And that was something she had sworn she would never do. Put herself in a position where she *had* to depend on someone, that is. And it seemed to be a triangle. Just as she depended on Frank, so Abby depended on *her*. And every minute of their association was drawing the knots tighter. She bent her head to avoid all the eyes staring at her.

'Yes,' she almost whispered, 'I would like you to be my lawyer.'

'And that settles that,' Mr Corey said brusquely. 'Now then, if you will sign this power of attorney. Right here please.' She inked the paper where he indicated, using his gold fountain pen. He looked it over, nodded his head, and smiled at her.

'Now we'll get to work,' he said. 'George, Harry—Bill? We'll be at the Hilton for tonight, Mother, and back here tomorrow.'

He was talking over Penny's head to his wife, who smiled as if she understood everything, and went back to her one-sided conversation with her granddaughter. Frank came around the table and leaned over to her. 'They're all going to Boston,' he said softly. 'I have some final business in Falmouth. I'll be back by noon. Please keep my mother company until then.'

Penny nodded agreement. He turned to his mother. 'Well?' he asked.

Mrs Corey gave him a big smile and patted the hand he rested on the back of her chair. 'Very well indeed,' she said. 'Now go about your business and leave us alone.'

'But——' Penny stuttered and cursed herself for her own weakness. 'Hey!' She yelled across the room, and waved her hand madly.

'You don't have to do that,' Mrs Corey told her. 'He'll be back. Frank was never one to leave a beautiful girl alone.'

'It's not Frank I'm concerned with,' Penny groaned. 'It's that—that waiter. He's stealing my breakfast! I haven't had two bites!'

'But I thought you had eaten before you came?'

Penny turned around and looked down at her. There was that lopsided grin that Frank wore—and now I know where it comes from, she told herself. 'I'm a big girl,' she sighed. 'It takes a lot to fill me up. I think I've been perpetually hungry for the last year!'

It was at that point that Penny received her first real instruction in what the Corey family was all about. His lovely mother, sophisticated, *chic*, dainty—put two fingers in her mouth and shrieked the loudest whistle that Penny had ever heard. The waiter stopped with one foot halfway to the floor and looked over his shoulder. One sweeping wave of the dowager's hand brought him back with the plate. The two women sat down at the table again. Mrs Corey ordered another cup of coffee. Abby, restless, spurred Penny to eat faster—even though the eggs were cold. They made conversation between bites.

'You must have led a fascinating life,' Penny tendered.

'Why? Because of the whistle? You learn that, my dear, when you have three boys and two girls in your family. You have to serve your time as a Den Mother, Campfire Leader, and then the Little League looms.

And of course you realise that I've been a Registered Nurse for years.'

'Oh Lord,' Penny groaned. 'Look at you all. Three—no—four lawyers in the family, and you've done all those things, and I'm just an unemployed nobody. You all make me feel very inadequate.'

'Don't you believe it,' the matriarch replied. 'We all started at the bottom of the heap. Maybe you're not intended for those sorts of careers. There's nothing wrong, you know, in being a mother and a housewife.' A moment of rumination. 'The pay's terrible of course—but there are other compensations. And I could teach you to whistle in twenty minutes.'

Three hours later the three of them had 'done' the village. Everything within walking distance, that is. They toured the Doll Museum, the Glass Museum and the Soldiers' Monument, all at the green; the old Grist Mill, once the heart of every colonial town, the home of America's famous Thornton Burgess, the author of the Peter Rabbit stories, and others. Heritage Plantation was beyond their foot capacity. It lay a mile or so more from the centre of town.

All of which brought them back, exhausted, to the Inn. Frank was waiting impatiently in the tavern. He set his beer aside as they walked past the door, and joined them as they put their feet up in the lounge.

'I thought I said noon?' he said gruffly as he took Penny's arm. Her first reaction was to shake him off, but better sense prevailed. Who knows, she told herself, whether he's in a mean mood or not!

'We were carried away,' she apologised.

'We was not,' Abby corrected her. 'We had to walk all the way. My feet hurt, Daddy.'

'There's not much I can do about that,' he said, but his tone had softened as he addressed his daughter. I wish he would talk to me that way, Penny thought, and was off in another dream. Vaguely she heard his mother step into the breach. 'You could buy us some lunch, Frank. And we need a place to rest our feet and get some of the dust off of us.'

'You needn't be concerned about me,' Penny offered. 'I'm used to this sort of life.'

'Nonsense,' Mrs Corey interrupted. 'Well, don't just stand there, son.'

'Now I'm the one who doesn't know what's going on,' he returned.

'Then I'll explain it,' his mother told him. 'First, go out to the front desk and get a room for Penny.'

'But we're not spending the night here, Mother.'

'What's that got to do with anything? Get Penny a room where she can freshen up, where she can put her feet up for a few minutes. And then you can order lunch for all of us. Is that too much to ask?'

The grim look on his face faded, and that half-grin played at his mouth. His eyes sparkled as Penny had not seen them do. He was a different person. He clicked his heels, laughing all the while. 'Yes, ma'am,' he conceded.

Her room was on the other side of a courtyard, in the Jarves Wing. It was a long way from the street, and quiet. Penny sprawled on the bed, ignoring the way her suit was bound to wrinkle. Frank had dropped his mother and Abby off at Room Ten, and then had led Penny down the long hall to the opposite end, Room Twenty. The porter who trailed them had unlocked the door, smiled when Frank's hand slipped something into his, and had gone. She stood in the open doorway, uncertain about what was next to come.

Something was, she had no doubt of that. An electric tension had built up between them during that slow sauntering walk. He brushed by her and went into the room. Almost as if hypnotised she followed him, closing the door behind her.

'Frank?' she questioned.

'Just looking, he said. He moved around the room, checked the view, the neatness of the attached bath, the spring of the bed. 'You know damn well I'm not just looking, don't you?'

'I don't know what I know,' she sighed. 'You hired me a lawyer, your mother walked me all over town, and I still don't know what's going on!'

'There's nothing to lose your temper about,' he commented. He came around the bed and stood close in front of her. She gradually backed away from him until she came up against the wall.

'I'm not losing my temper—yet,' she told him. 'But it won't be too much longer, Frank Corey.'

He closed the distance between them, trapping her by putting a hand on either side of her. He's too close, her alarm system told her.

'My mother likes you,' he said. She gulped. Obviously she had missed something. Somewhere along the line, when she should have caught a clue, she had missed it. And now this.

'I like her too,' she said very firmly. 'Does that signify?'

'It means that you're a girl who's easy to like.'

'I don't think so. I lived with Uncle Henry for six years, and he never liked me.'

'Which is a mystery we'll clean up very quickly. My father likes you too, by the way. My mother likes all the cuddly little girls I bring home. My father, he likes what he likes.'

'I—I don't understand what you're saying. Should you be here with me like this?'

'You're worried about us being alone in a hotel room, when we've been living on top of each other out on the Lane?'

'Well, it's—I don't know what it is. What's going on, Frank? I don't really understand, and I want to.'

'You will, lady,' he chuckled. His head bent those few inches needed, blotting out the sunlight. She closed her eyes, tense, expectant. Nothing happened. Disappointed, she opened one eye. His face was so close to hers that only his nose was in focus. He chuckled, and travelled that last inch or two.

It was as before, only better. She closed her eyes

again and stood perfectly still while his lips sealed hers in a welcome communion of spirit and flesh. A gentle pressure, full of moist promise, and then his arms came around her. The pressure increased and she could feel the violence of her own reaction. Deep within her, starting almost from her weakened knees, a riot of pleasure swept up her spine and spread in all directions. Little countercycles were formed where his wandering hands touched. Her arms crept up to him, surrounded him, and she clung with all the passion of an unawakened soul. The bliss of it all has become addictive, her mind shouted at her. No matter what happens between us, she replied, I shall never feel with any other man what I feel with Frank! But it was no time for thought. The sensations went on and on until, out of breath, she squirmed slightly in his grasp, and he loosened his hold.

'That's part of the puzzle,' he said, stepping back from her. She followed, still clinging to her hold around his neck. He let her hang there, suspended by her emotions, not her hands. And then finally he unwrapped her grip and forced her arms back to her sides. 'And that's another clue,' he chuckled. 'I think that's all you can take just now!'

The words, the gesture, broke the spell. 'Oh you— you rotten, egotistical, arrogant——' She managed to free one hand and swung in the general direction of his head. He ducked out of the way, caught both her hands in one of his, and began to retreat towards the door, laughing all the way. It wasn't until he was safely out in the hall that he released her, pushing her back inside and closing the door between them.

'Twenty minutes,' he called through the door, 'And not a minute later if you want lunch.'

'Huh!' she snorted, but not loudly enough to be heard in the hall. 'Some day, man! Some day I'll get you!' And she had thrown herself down on the bed, half-crying, half-laughing. 'He's right,' she thought. 'I don't have a clue. What kind of a girl am I? I thought virgins were supposed to be patient and passive. And every time he gets close I just want to jump on him! Well, I'll be more attentive in the future!' Damn that man! She rolled over on the bed and checked her watch. Twenty minutes? There was time for ten minutes worth of dreaming before she had to wash.

CHAPTER SEVEN

IN the end it was three days before the Corey men came back from Boston. And there had been changes. For one thing, Abby had gone. 'Back to Northampton,' Frank told her, 'with her grandmother. It's been her home for most of her life, and my mother decided it would be better to take her home.'

Penny heard all this at the end of that first day, when he drove her back to Navigation Lane. There was no speaking of plans. When it was time to go Abby had just disappeared, and Penny had felt that desolate coldness creep over her, the cold which had surrounded her before she met—Frank. The cold of loneliness. Frank himself seemed to be preoccupied. He handed her out of the Mercedes, escorted her to her front door, and stopped there.

'You'll be all right, Penny,' he said. 'There aren't any more ghosts haunting the Neck to spy on you. I've arranged for a couple of friends of mine in the police service to keep an eye on you. And I'll see you later sometime.'

He was gone before she could protest. No kiss, no hug, not even a warm squeeze of her hand. She stood stiffly at her door and watched while he reversed the car out on to the lane and roared off. He didn't even wave as he went, she told herself. And that's certainly a lesson for you, stupid!

She rattled around the house, disturbing the dust with a cloth, stripping Abby's bed and piling the sheets in her laundry basket. She hardly felt like eating. The lovely lunch at the Inn had been enough to just sustain her through the afternoon. The omelette she made for supper looked edible while in the pan, but when placed on the table it lost all its attraction. In the end she satisfied herself with a piece of toast and two more mugs of coffee.

The October night sky was brilliant, but cold winds whistled off the bay; too cold for her to wander down the Marsh road, or even to sit out behind the house. Wrapped in a misery she could not define, she stumbled upstairs for a warm bath, and was in bed by nine o'clock.

Sleep eluded her. 'I miss Abby,' she kept telling herself, which was only half the truth. She missed them both. She had only to close her eyes to find his face staring at her. My princely Galahad, she laughed wryly. Lord, not only is he not a Galahad, but he isn't mine, either. In the faint rays of pre-dawn she finally fell into a fitful sleep.

The day passed in a daze. She managed a piece of toast and a mug of coffee, then dawdled around, giving the kitchen cabinets the half-swipe she had been promising for weeks. Then, with nothing but four walls to stare at, she shrugged into her fleece-lined shortcoat, and went out. The sun was playing peek-a-boo with a heavy line of black clouds. The few high tufts of marsh grass which had escaped the reapers were bent almost double. She could hear the roar of the breakers as they smashed up on the outer beaches. It definitely was not a day for beachcombing. Wearily she cast about in her mind for something to do. Go to the bank, for one, and transfer money from her savings to her checking account!

Before she could find some other reason for procrastination she jumped into the van and struggled down to the Cape Cod Cooperative bank, which shared a small Mall area with the Post Office. After all, even the most inexperienced clerk can hardly find it difficult to transfer three hundred dollars from one account to another. And so back to the van and a leisurely drive down to the house.

The storm was still threatening. She parked the vehicle in the drive, mustered up her courage, and went for a walk down into the Marshes. The lane, bad enough up at the house, deteriorated as it dropped to the level of the Marsh. She thrust her hands into her pockets, kicked a little stone ahead of her, and opened her ears to the life around her. The tide was going out, and the Marsh was draining. Not in one great flood down some creek, but by thousands of little rivulets that gradually worked their way to the ocean. The black clouds, spreading, matched her mood. She turned back and retraced her path to the house.

Over a cup of coffee in the kitchen she tried again to analyse her own feelings. First there was the little girl. Abigail Corey. She had no argument with Abby, the girl needed no one to plead her case. Just one look at her elfin face was enough. Do you, Penny Harris, love Abigail Corey? 'Indeed I do,' she muttered. And that was part one, argument and conclusion. I love Abby Corey.

Part two, there is this man. Not overwhelmingly tall, although he has muscles aplenty. Homely as the day is long—and yet, to be honest, he isn't all *that* ugly. We're not talking about Quasimodo, the Hunchback of Notre-Dame! And he's improving! Gradually and strangely, he's getting better looking all the time! He has a host of problems. He has a strange sense of humour. He's arrogant and conceited. He wants to be a dictator. He cherishes information like a clam, so there's no way of knowing what the devil he's up to. He *says* he's a lawyer, and his dad says the same, so perhaps he is. He loves his mother and does what she tells him. He loves his daughter. He doesn't want to be my lawyer. His daughter loves him. Me too!

Game, set, and match. What now? The question hung in the air as she fumbled around for something more to eat, and then trailed upstairs to bath and bed. For the first time since she had moved into the lane, she was sorry she had no television. She turned on the radio. WCIB boomed in on her with music from the fifties.

She let it blare, and hardly noticed it was still on when she dropped off to sleep.

The next day passed as had the first. But this time she spent the whole morning in bed, catching up on the paperback titles she had accumulated but not read. It helped. The afternoon was more difficult to deal with. She went down to her kitchen, resolved to make bread. It was a total failure, but she marked it down in her memory. Item: when things—when we settle the Foundation, I must go to a cooking school. Ahead of her she could see endlessly long days stretching into infinity, when she would have to live off her own cooking. By nightfall she had managed to clean the utensils. Why didn't it rise, she asked herself as she crouched over the cook book, checking off ingredients. Yeast! Dear lord, everything but the yeast! She slammed the book shut and hurled it against the wall. The storm that had been threatening for two days broke at that very instant. The wind rose to a banshee wail, and great drops of rain slanted sidewise against the house, bounding off walls and windows, threatening to get at her. They can't get in, she screamed to herself. It's only a storm. She ran up the stairs, huddled in bed, and pulled the covers over her head.

All of which brought her to day three tired, dishevelled, shaken, and looking like death warmed over. And that was, of course, the time he came. He bustled into the house without let or leave, thumped across the living-room to the kitchen, and paused at the door. She raised her pale tear-streaked face to him.

'My God,' he pronounced. 'You look as if you've been in a fight with a mountain lion—and lost.'

'Thank you,' she sighed despondently. 'Your friends speak well of you too. Both of them. Is there some reason why you've burst into my house?'

He refused to rise to the bait. 'You don't get me into any fights today, little lady. Get on your best bib and tucker. They're all back, and its time for a council of war.'

'No thanks,' she moaned. 'Start the war without me.'

'My, we *are* feeling sorry for ourselves, aren't we!'

'I don't know about you, but surely I am. The door opens outward. I'd be pleased if you didn't slam it after you.'

'You're giving up in the middle of the race,' he chuckled. 'Come on now, rustle upstairs and get dressed. Your lawyer is waiting for you at the Inn.'

'Not me,' she said angrily. 'I've had enough.'

'You've got thirty minutes to get yourself upstairs and dressed,' he threatened. 'Or else!'

'Or else what?'

'Or else I'll do it for you,' he snapped. 'God protect me from women like you! Entirely wrapped up in yourself, aren't you!'

'Why you rotten, arrogant——'

'Now there's only twenty-eight minutes. Going?'

'I'm not afraid of you,' she snarled. And just to prove it, she went upstairs to dress. And I'm *not* afraid of him, she told herself. Not the tiniest bit. I'm only doing this—out of respect for his father, that's what. And his mother. She hardly had time to comb out her hair, but she did manage a little pale pink lipstick, a dab of mascara on those already heavy lashes, and the smallest bit of light eyeshadow. When she sauntered downstairs, still intent on proving she was not afraid of him, there were ten seconds left to go.

'I suppose that's the best I can expect,' he told her. 'Pink lipstick?'

'Yes. Have you got something against pink?'

'I don't mind,' he said. 'Does it kiss off?'

'I—yes—I mean—I don't know,' she stuttered. 'Why do you always come up with these fool statements about—watch what you're doing!' The last part of the statement ended in a squeak of alarm as he very competently demonstrated that the pink was not kissproof.

'Now what did you do that for?' she stormed at him. 'Now I'll have to do it all over again!'

'Me too,' he said solemnly as he handed her into the Mercedes. She moved as far away from him as she could get. 'Would you want to ride in the back seat?' he asked sarcastically.

'I don't know what I want,' she returned grimly. 'Every time I see you I have the urge to scratch your eyes out.'

'Don't think I haven't noticed,' he laughed. 'I take it you didn't enjoy my absence?'

'I missed Abby,' she answered. 'I missed her very much.'

'And me?'

'I—why would I miss *you*?' she snarled. 'All you ever bring is trouble.'

'How wrong they are,' he laughed. 'Did you know my mother said that with a little training you'd make a sweet, biddable wife?'

'Maybe, but not for you. I don't know when I've ever found a man whom I despise so much. Why, I——' For some reason she was crying, something that she hardly ever did. At least she never had done so until she met this—this man! She huddled in her corner and let the tears flow. He wisely left her alone, although he slowed the car noticeably. A traffic line was forming behind them when she managed to shut off the deluge. He handed her a huge handkerchief. She dabbed at her eyes.

'You—you just make me so damn mad!'

'I know,' he said solemnly. 'You have that effect on me, too. Better now?' He patted her knee. Where ordinarily she might have hit him for it, now she took comfort.

'Yes,' she said quietly. And then, 'I had a miserable day yesterday. And the day before.'

'Ah well.' It seemed as if he might say something else, but by then they had arrived at the side portico of the Dan'l Webster Inn, and it was too late to reconstruct the mood. He shut off the engine, set the parking brake, and came around to hold her door. The other Corey men were waiting in the lounge, sitting comfortably around a low coffee table. Drinks and papers covered its surface. They all stood as she came in. Frank helped her to a seat and then sat down beside her.

'Miss Harris,' the older man, Michael Corey, said.

'Penny, please,' she insisted. He gave her a courtly nod.

'Penny, we've done as much research as possible in so short a time. I'm ready now to recapitulate your position.'

She waved an assent. Frank, who had momentarily disappeared, popped up again, setting a glass in front of her. She sniffed at it. 'Brandy?'

'Yes. Drink it down.'

'The news is so bad I'm going to need it?' He patted her hand. She took a sip and set it aside. 'I'd prefer to have it cold turkey,' she told them all.

'The only way to go,' Frank's father said. 'The music plays like this. According to the terms of your grandfather's will, the Board of Directors of the Foundation has the absolute right to make any disposition of funds that they desire.'

'So they can dissolve the Foundation?'

'At their next meeting, if a majority favours it. Now, your grandfather arranged things so that control is determined by the number of shares each member of the Board holds, just as with any profit-making corporation. Your Uncle Henry, acting as your guardian, has voting control over five thousand shares. The remainder, twenty thousand shares, is held in trust by the Bank of Boston. They have no voting rights. Their only interest is to hand this twenty thousand shares over to you under either one of two conditions. The first is when you reach your twenty-first birthday. I understand that takes place in January?'

'January the twenty-fourth,' she sighed. 'Too late to halt the vote?'

'Yes, too late. The final vote will be taken on November fifteenth. It's been properly advertised in accordance with the bylaws, and everything is on the up and up.'

'Then I've lost?'

'Not exactly, my dear.' They all leaned forward around the table pinning her in place with their eyes. 'There is one other provision of the will,' Mr Corey continued. 'If you marry, you may immediately take control of your shares and do whatever you want to at the next election.'

'And I have no other choices?'

'None at all, my dear. It's up to you.'

'I'd like to talk to Penny alone,' Frank interrupted. 'Why don't you all stay and finish your drinks while we take a stroll?' She looked up at him as he took her arm; that grim look was back on his face. A shiver ran down her spine as he pulled her up.

'What is it, Frank?'

'In a minute,' he said through clenched teeth. He walked her out into the lobby, empty at this time of day. When he was sure they were alone he turned around to face her. 'How badly do you really want that forty million dollars?' he grated.

She looked away from him. How much did she want it? Not at all. But there were all of Grandpa's dreams. All the things he had told her over the years, time after time, engraving them on her young mind. It was Grandfather's money, and she was the only one who knew what he wanted done with it. But what would all that mean to Frank?

She squared her shoulders and looked up at him. 'I want that money very much,' she said firmly. 'Very, very much!'

He nodded as if he had expected that answer. The grim look was fixed more deeply on his face. 'Then you have only ten days to act,' he reminded her.

She shook her head. There was no way she could see what he saw. Her face was flushed and determined, her eyes flashing, her hair escaping from the scarf she had thrown over it, and hanging down almost over her face.

Even her tall lithe figure bespoke determination. He sighed, a deep rattling sigh. 'In that case, Penny, I would like you to marry me.'

'I—but——' she spluttered. He took her by the arm and urged her back to the lounge. 'What other way is there?' he asked. 'What other man do you know who might marry you in a hurry?'

'No—nobody,' she gasped, 'but——'

'But here I am. We're well acquainted. Abby is a favourite of yours. You like my family. And you want the money badly, don't you?'

'Yes, I do,' she stammered. 'But—being married is a big step for a woman, Frank.' And what can you possibly mean, that we're well acquainted? The only thing I really know about you is that I love you! And where does that leave me in the face of such a cold-blooded proposal?

'I know that,' he muttered. 'But this wedding will be under extraordinary circumstances. So I'm not the best-looking man who ever chased you, and you *are*—one of the most beautiful women I've ever met.'

'Huh!' she sniffed. 'Don't try to make this a Beauty and the Beast thing. That won't fly, Frank.'

A brief, wintry smile broke through the lines of his face. 'Thank God for that,' he said. 'Well, what do you say?'

'I—I don't know what to say. Everything you say is correct, but I——'

'But you miss the romance, the Hunter's Moon, the bended knee, the long white dress?'

Yes, she screamed to herself, I miss all that! I'm a romantic fool, and I'll miss all that. But if I say no, I'll miss what I really want in all the world. Marry my love, and do what grandfather wanted. Should I turn it down now just because he doesn't love me? At least we'd be sexually compatible, and I've heard that that's three-quarters of any successful marriage. So why am I diddling? 'Yes, Frank, I'll marry you.'

He nodded again, just as if the answer were

inevitable. His father and brothers looked up from their long yellow foolscap pads, and then stood to welcome them. Frank told them of their decision. His father's face lit up like a lighthouse; his two brothers pounded him on the back and lined up to kiss the prospective bride. But there was more on Michael Corey's mind than well wishes.

'How soon?' he asked. 'Time is of the essence.'

'Four days,' Frank returned. 'There's no quicker way. Massachusetts absolutely requires a blood test before issuing a licence. Today's Friday. If we get the tests done today, the weekend shuts everything down. So that means the closest we can do would be next Wednesday.' They all immediately consulted pocket calendars. 'So that means October the twenty-fifth. Six more days in October, fourteen in November.'

'Plenty of time,' their father replied. 'Now you, Frank, go call your mother and explain it. The rest of you scoot out of here. It's time I had a confidential talk with my client.'

'I think she had better come with me first,' Frank protested. 'You know how Mother will react. And I don't need to get in her books any worse than I am already.' His father smiled and waved them out. Once again Frank's arm was under her elbow as he moved her along at full speed, back to Room Twenty.

'We held the room,' he told her as he unlocked the door. 'And it makes a convenient place from which to phone.' He motioned her to a chair as he picked up the instrument and established his call to Northampton. His mother answered on the first ring. Penny could hear her voice plainly, although the telephone was two feet or more away from her.

'Why, I was just thinking of you,' his mother said. 'I've been sitting here for an hour trying to get up the courage to give you a call. What's the news?'

'What you wanted,' he laughed. 'Penny has agreed to marry me.' He held the receiver away from his ear at the resulting shriek of excitement. When finally his mother had calmed down he resumed his side of the conversation. 'Well, it only happened fifteen minutes ago, so I could hardly have called you earlier, could I?'

His mother was pacified. Her voice-level dropped, and Penny could no longer make out what she was saying. That is, up until the point when Frank put the cat among the pigeons. 'No,' he said abruptly. 'We will *not* be coming home for a grand wedding in the Corey style. We have to be married immediately. I've decided on a civil wedding. It will be next Wednesday, down here. Judge Simpson has agreed to perform the ceremony in his chambers.'

His mother almost screamed, but Penny had lost track. A civil ceremony. He has already made the arrangements. And there went all her dreams of long white dresses, bridal veils and orange blossoms. And he didn't even *ask* me. He didn't even *ask*! No indeed. 'I've decided.' Well he might want to start married life that way, but he was due for some big surprises if he expected her to be a floor mat for him!

'She wants to talk to you!' He waved the telephone in her face. She mustered a rather frigid smile on her face, and took the instrument in her hand.

'Penny? I'm so happy—for you, and for Frank. You're just the sort of girl he needs, but I'm astonished at his silly ideas about the wedding. You surely are going to put your foot down?'

'No, ma'am,' she said softly. Her mind was running at full speed, and she intended to make a good impression. 'Whatever Frank wants is all right with me. I hope you won't be disappointed?'

'In a way yes, in a way no,' his mother returned. 'I'd love to dress a bride—it's been a family tradition which I hate to break. But if it will get my poor ugly duckling married, why I'm all for it. By the way, you should call me *Mother* now.'

'But—all right, Mother. But he's not, you know.'

'Not what?'

'He's not your ugly duckling.'

'Why of course not,' Mrs Corey laughed. 'Now he's *your* ugly duckling. Congratulations to you both, and I expect to see you here at home right after the wedding.'

'I don't know about—right after—Mother.' The word had a marvellous taste to it. The simplest word in the dictionary, and she had never used it before. 'I—I think we have to go to Boston for a time, and I don't really know how soon.'

'I understand. When he gets through calling himself your lawyer, you must call him Papa. All the girls do. Go about your business, love, while I talk some more sense into that—into my son.'

Penny watched Frank for a moment. That smile was continually playing around his mouth, turning him into a man of splendour—there was no other word for it. Her face turned beet-red when he looked up and caught her looking. She scampered out of the room, back down the hall to where her lawyer was waiting for her, nursing a small drink in his hands.

'Now then, young lady,' he said, 'I've been watching you for some time. Every single mention of that forty million dollars, and I can see a scheming light in those eyes of yours. So before we go overboard, tell me just what you plan to do with the money.'

She watched his eyes. The windows to the soul, someone had written. If so, Michael Corey's soul was in good shape. So she took a deep breath, and told him in great detail exactly what she wanted done with the money. When Frank came back to get her he found his prospective bride sitting with an amazingly large smile on her face, while his father was doubled over, laughing so hard that his stomach muscles were aching. And neither of them would explain *anything* to him!

Frank put up with it for about five minutes, then tapped his father on the shoulder. 'You think that's funny,' he snapped. 'Let me tell you something that's *really* funny. Your wife is coming down from Northampton tomorrow to supervise the wedding!'

And so she did. She arrived by car at the Inn before

ten o'clock. Frank had already arranged to take Penny in to Barnstable to arrange for blood tests and a marriage licence. They need now only wait the prerequisite days until Wednesday.

'I have the ring,' he told his mother, 'and the witnesses, so there's nothing more to be done.'

'A lot you know,' his mother told him. 'Is she to be married in her dungarees? The child must be outfitted. It may be only a small civil wedding, but the bride expects to be treated as a bride, Frank Corey.'

'All right.' He surrendered without a shot. 'Do whatever you need to do, but don't bother me about it.'

'But I—I need to speak to you privately,' Penny told Mrs Corey. The older woman took one look at her worried face, and lead her out into the lobby to find a vacant corner. They settled in a deep-cushioned couch. Penny found herself unable to begin.

'It can't be all that bad,' his mother told her. One of those small but efficient hands came over and patted Penny's. 'Just spit it all out.'

'I—I know you've heard all this conversation about my forty million dollars,' Penny started off. The other woman nodded her head. 'Well, it really isn't mine. My grandfather left it for something else. I don't have any control over it, and all the money I have is what I've earned. I just don't have enough money to buy any clothes. I've got one or two nice dresses at home—but that has to be it. And I can't let Frank pay for—well, I just can't.'

'No, I could see that,' Mrs Corey returned. 'But then again, you wouldn't want to shame him at his wedding, would you?'

'Oh no,' Penny sighed, 'I wouldn't. But there's nothing I can do about it.'

'Of course there is, my dear. It's the prerogative of the bride's mother to buy the wedding gown.'

'But—I don't have a mother.'

'You have me, my dear.' Which was all too much for Penny, already strung tighter than a violin's E string, to handle. The tears came, oceans of them. Somehow or another she found herself resting on the shoulder of this tiny, wonderful woman, and crying her heart out. Frank came into the lobby to enquire, but was waved off by his mother, and disappeared. And the next day, with all the tears dried, the two women went shopping. They were looking for something simple, which takes a great deal longer than finding something fancy.

They finally found what they wanted, way down in South Orleans, at the Twice As Nice shop. It was a delightful, light-as-a-breeze, two-piece dress, in pure white silk. The top had extended shoulders with a two-inch fringe and a blousoned waist. The skirt, just slightly below the knee, was pleated, with an elasticated band at the waist. The neck was cool and demure, and it cost only a third again as much as Penny's entire savings. Mrs Corey pooh-poohed the whole idea of expense, and demanded a pair of shoes to match.

A simple idea, shoes, but it occasioned another hour of search. Everything that matched the dress had four-inch heels, and Penny was bound and determined she was not going to stand taller than Frank at *his* wedding. And what a silly idea that is, she lectured herself as she followed Mrs Corey from store to store. *His* wedding! *My* wedding is what it is, and I'll wear what I please! None of which explained why, despite her companion's objections, she bought a pair of white open-toed flats. There was no discussion about veils, and Penny vetoed the hat. The cost of the day had already chilled her. They drove back to the Inn, where Mrs Corey was now installed 'For the Duration,' she said.

'And Abby will be down on Tuesday,' she also said. 'I hated to take her out of school again, considering how much she's missed, but I did think—you know—for her father's wedding? And the Principal did agree. Mrs Rathers, you'll remember.'

'How could I forget,' Frank returned. He was looking more and more harassed every minute, and it made Penny feel uneasy.

'And then after the wedding,' Mrs Corey ploughed on, 'you'll be the one to decide such things, Penny.'

'Mother!'

'Don't turn up your nose at me, Frank,' his mother snapped. 'It's true. Once you're married, Abby becomes your wife's responsibility, and I look forward to making the change. I love her very much, but I'm not young enough to be dealing with a girl that age. Now then, what are you up to, young lady?'

'Well, it *is* late,' Penny sighed. 'I thought I would be going back home now, and——'

'Home? You refer to the house on—what was that lane?'

'Navigation Lane,' her son responded. 'I'll drive Penny over, and then come back.'

'Why, of course,' his mother said. 'And I'll come with you just to get a peek at this place. You *did* say you lived next door, Frank?'

'Yes I did, Mother. For a time, you understand. But you wouldn't want to see it. It's down in the marshes, and not at all what you——'

'Frank Corey, I do believe you're getting hard of hearing. I distinctly said I *did* want to see it. Now, let's get on our way, or I'll miss the very fine buffet they've been advertising for supper tonight.'

It was with some apprehension that Penny crowded into the front seat of the Mercedes, squeezed between Frank and his mother. 'I could easily sit in the back,' she protested.

'Not at all,' Mrs Corey told her. 'There's plenty of room.' And indeed there was, except that her thigh brushed hard against Frank's, and she could feel his muscles tense as he moved his foot up and down on the pedal. It made breathing a little harder, but was not the worst part of the operation. For some reason, whenever he swung the wheel to the left his right elbow would come up and gently indent her breast. And *that* was something that was hard to stand. Not painful— just teasing. By the time they arrived at the house Penny was at the exasperating stage of being sexually excited, and unable to do anything about it.

They drove up into the yard and stopped a few feet from the houses. Mrs Corey sat very still for a moment, studying both forlorn buildings. 'You live here?' she asked. The disbelief in her voice could hardly be misunderstood.

'Yes,' Penny said stiffly. 'And I'm darned lucky to be able to find a place like this. It's hard to find a place to live on the Cape. I got it for a yearly rental, mind you, not one of these summertime leases.'

'I see,' his mother said. 'I think I would like to look inside.' She opened her door and climbed out. Penny squirmed across the seat and followed. The fat's in the fire now, she told herself. The outside is bad enough. Wait until she sees the inside! But the lady from Northampton was not to be discouraged. She followed hard on Penny's heels up to the front door and into the living-room. She stopped in the middle of the room and turned slowly, taking in every cranny and corner, every hole in the carpet, every scar on the chairs, and the accumulated dust on the coffee table. She even walked over to the table and ran her gloved finger across its surface.

Oh lord, Penny wailed to herself, she's giving it the old Army white-glove inspection! Do all mother-in-laws do that? There must be some way I can distract her! 'The kitchen is this way,' she essayed. 'We do all our—I mean, I do all of my living in the kitchen.'

'Do you indeed,' Mrs Corey said, and followed her through to the kitchen. At least here Penny felt more secure. Everything was in its place, all the dishes were done, the table sparkled with polish, and even the garbage can was sanitary. The inspecting lady went directly to the sink. Once gleaming white enamel, it had seen better days. Chipped here and there, it resembled a mosaic in some ruined Greek temple, rather than the pride of modern plumbing. And those gloved fingers were stroking the chipped areas.

'I guess you wouldn't want to see upstairs,' Penny asked hopefully.

'Oh, but I would,' Mrs Corey responded. 'Indeed I would.'

Penny led the way upstairs like the leading Christian on the way up to the Colosseum. The rooms were clean, the beds all made with fresh linen, the bathroom sparkled as much as elbow grease could make it, but— but it was all so dingy. And Mrs Corey did the inconceivable. She turned on the faucet and watched while the rusty water gushed into the tub. She turned it off.

'This will never do, Frank,' she told him. 'You can't expect a nice girl like Penny to be married from such a—slum.'

'But I——'

The matriarch held up her hand. 'It's plain to see you've done wonders keeping this place up,' she said, 'but it's obviously not worth the effort. Frank?'

'Well, we could take her back to the Inn,' he suggested. His mother beamed. 'The very idea,' she said.

'But I can't,' Penny wailed. 'You know I can't, Mrs Corey.'

'Call me Mother, dear. Yes you can. Have you a suitcase? Go pack your things, child. Frank, go downstairs and see if there are things to be shut off. The gas, for example. Penny won't be coming back here.'

'But my lease is good until January the thirty-first,' Penny objected. 'I——'

That imperious hand was raised again. Stop, it said. Why do I let myself be ordered around by that tiny woman? she asked herself. What does she have that I haven't? Confidence, for one thing.

She was startled to hear some close-by voice saying, 'Yes ma'am, I'll pack my bag.'

She wandered across the hall to her own bedroom. Mrs Corey followed. Penny struggled to get her bag down. She had jammed it hard in the upper shelf, not expecting to use it too soon. It came out with a plop, and dozens of little things she had long forgotten fell off the shelf after it. Shaking her head, she opened the bag on her bed, and began to transfer her meagre wardrobe out of the wardrobe. It took very little time.

'Travelling light, were you?' His mother had pre-empted the only chair in the room, and was slowly rocking back and forth.

'Yes,' Penny sighed. 'I suppose you know I—had to run away.'

'I know, dear. My husband and I share everything. What you tell him you tell me, and vice versa. It takes an open exchange to keep a marriage sweet.'

Penny closed the suitcase. The lock was broken, so she didn't bother with it. Instead she turned and looked at the older woman. 'I wish I knew something about marriage,' she said softly. 'I've never seen one working. I mean, I've never been close enough to married people to see how they go on from day to day. And I need to know. Frank is—for me—very hard to know.'

'Just what do you know about him?' his mother asked.

Penny wrinkled her brow, and threw caution to the winds. 'The only thing I know is that I love him,' she admitted. 'And I don't think that's enough. Do you?'

'I don't claim to be an expert,' Mrs Corey laughed. 'I've only been married once. But Michael and I have been together for forty-two years. And no, you don't know enough. There are lots of days to get through, my dear, and they can't all be borne along by passion. It takes more sharing than that. Day to day little things. But you'll learn those as you go along.'

'But I don't even know enough about him to make conversation after the wedding,' Penny pleaded. 'Tell me at least a little something. Like, why is Frank so—so homely, when his father and you and his brothers are all so—so handsome.'

'Ah. He wouldn't tell you that,' his mother said softly. 'Frank is my baby boy, you know. He was the best-looking of them all. He went to Vietnam with his Reserve fighter squadron.'

'Oh dear! I didn't know. He had an—an accident?'

'He had been married a year before he went off,' Mrs Corey went on doggedly. 'Abby was born after he left. He came back with his face completely destroyed. They actually had to rebuild him. And his wife took one look at him and ran off with an anti-war protestor. It left him—well—bitter. He still has emotional highs and lows due to his military service. You'll notice that. He needs careful handling and a firm hand. Be gentle with him. He needs someone to love him just for himself.'

'I'll try,' Penny said pensively. 'If he'll let me.'

CHAPTER EIGHT

PENNY had heard about marriages that were made in heaven or hell, but in a judge's office? It somehow reminded her of her first job interview, when she had applied for a secretary's position, and found that 'no experience' was the password to a quick exit. Almost any minute, she told herself, Judge Simpson will turn around to me and say, 'And how much experience do you have, Miss Harris?' And that would be the end of the wedding! She shivered and then clung tightly to Frank's arm. He was the only stable thing in the room. He and Abby, standing at her side, dressed somehow in a gown identical to the one Penny herself was wearing.

The judge was in a hurry. He took time to examine the licence, smiled at Frank like an old friend, and was off from the starting gate, reciting the marriage lines as if he were calling the third race at Hialeah Race Track. But no matter that it sounded all gibberish to her, Frank seemed to know exactly what was going on. He nodded in all the right places, prodded her when she missed her cue to speak, and then, when it was over, kissed her chastely on the brow, as if he thought she might break if he touched her.

The ring on her finger was terribly heavy. Solid gold, a wide band, suitable to share a finger with the garish diamond he had given her the day before. She squirmed around and looked sidelong at it. With gold quoted at over four hundred dollars an ounce, this certainly cost a pretty penny. Oh God, what a terrible pun!

She did look pretty. She knew that, just as she knew it was someone else, wearing her body.

'Smile,' Frank urged in her ear. 'Happy is the bride, and all that.'

'Yes, sure,' she moaned. 'I'm going to cry. Get me out of here!'

He tucked his hand under her arm and swept her through the group. It seemed like a crowd, although it was only his father and mother and his three brothers, and his sister Ethel. *Now I wish I'd worn a veil,* she stormed at herself as the tears formed. They rushed out of the low Probate building behind the old stone court house. Abby was right behind them, tugging at the hem of Penny's dress. She squeezed back her tears and took control of herself. *The little girl's problems must have first priority,* she told herself. *That's why he married me.*

'And now I can call you Mama?' Abby looked up hesitantly.

'If you want,' Penny managed. The girl's face broke out in a massive smile. *Like her father,* Penny thought, but ever so much more endearing. She half-knelt on the stair of the court house and offered an embrace. 'Oh Mommy!' The child was at the tearful stage herself; they both let the rivulets flow, each crying for a different reason. Frank stood there, astonished. When she stood up, bringing the child up in her arms, she could see the look on his face. Surprise, doubt, astonishment – and something else she could not classify. His father and mother came out behind them.

'Hey, none of that,' Mr Corey chuckled. 'The honeymoon's over. I need to talk to my client.'

'But—but——' Penny stuttered.

'I guess you don't get a honeymoon,' Abby said solemnly. 'But if you do, can I come too?'

Without thinking, she answered. 'Of course you can, love. We're a family now, aren't we?'

'Yes,' Frank said. His voice had icicles hanging from each word. That grim look was back on his face. 'I'll take Abby back to the Inn. You go with my father, and join us when you can. You're in Room Twenty again.'

The conference with her father-in-law took almost three hours. First there was a long debate. He wanted to be exactly sure what she wanted done. Then there was a pause while he rounded up a secretary, and another two hours for a dozen and one forms to be filled out and signed. When the papers were finished they were handed to George, who left immediately for Boston. It was six o'clock before everything was done. Penny beamed with satisfaction.

'You're sure it will work?' she asked hesitantly.

'Perfectly sure,' he laughed. 'Why else would you be paying me such a fantastic amount of money?'

She was swept up by his enthusiasm. 'But now I wish I hadn't paid you a whole dollar,' she teased. 'I went out with your wife and spent every other penny I own. That leaves me with – eighty-five cents.'

'That's what husbands are for,' he advised. 'Go put the bee on Frank.'

'Oh—I—I couldn't do that,' she affirmed, putting both hands to her hot cheeks. 'Every time I mention money to Frank he gets so mad that I—well, I just can't.'

'Then I'll tell you what we'll do,' Mr Corey said. 'As your lawyer I can advance you something based on the settlement of the case. How about five hundred dollars?'

'You could do that?'

'Of course. All perfectly legal, my dear.' He whipped out his fountain pain again and rapidly scribbled out a cheque for her. 'Try that on for size. Guaranteed not to bounce. Do not fold, hook or mutilate.'

'Can I ask you another question?'

'As your lawyer?'

'I—I guess as my father-in-law.'

'Then the answer is yes, you can ask without charge. What's the question?'

'Well, Frank's a lawyer too, and you know what's to happen to *my* money. Do lawyers make enough money to afford a large family?'

'That all depends,' he chuckled. 'It does my heart good. Do you intend to have a large family?'

She ducked her head to hide the blush. 'Yes,' she sighed. And then hastily, 'But we haven't talked about anything like that and I don't know what he'll think, but if we can——'

'The answer is yes,' he returned. 'Frank is one hell of a lawyer. He can make enough money to support you and your large family in any style you want. Satisfied?'

'I——' she stammered, and then leaned closer to him. 'You're a very nice man,' she told him, stretching to kiss his cheek. 'If I hadn't met Frank first, well——'

'How about that!' He tilted his courtly head to one side and smiled down at her. 'I hope, child, that most of your dreams come true. It's tempting Fate to think that they *all* might make it, but I hope that it's *most*, at least. Now, we've been at this foolishness long enough. Off you go to get cleaned up. And don't nibble on anything. I'm standing for the dinner tonight, and then the rest of us are heading out.'

'Oh my——' She reached for his arm to hold him. 'You won't tell Frank—promise me you won't ever tell Frank about the money!'

'I promise, my love. Not under any circumstance.' She smiled thankfully.

'And are you all going back to Northampton tonight?'

'No. Only the noncombatants. Mother and Abby and Ethel, to be exact. The boys and I will be spending the next few days in Boston.'

'Should I come with you?'

'Not at all, Penny. This show will work best if you're a complete surprise to them. When we walk into that Boardroom on the fifteenth, I want to hear them all gasp for breath. After which the execution begins. I'll be back here on the fourteenth, and you and I will drive up directly to the meeting.'

'And the others?'

'I'll contact everybody you've mentioned in the next few days. Don't worry about it. Scoot now.' He dropped a gentle kiss on her forehead and pushed her into the waiting car. She could hardly wait. It had been almost four hours since she had seen her 'husband', and the name took some getting used to. She stopped just long enough in the lobby of the Inn to get her key, and zoomed down the hallways as fast as her long shapely legs would take her. The hall was quiet and empty. She fumbled the key into the lock of Room Twenty, twisted it, and flung open the door. The room was quiet and empty.

She faltered, not wanting to enter if he were not there. Hung up between choices, she finally noticed how rumpled her dress had become. The flowers that his mother had bought for her were wilted, and surely her face needed re-doing. Which was enough of an incentive to bring her into the room. Behind the closed door she looked around. Her one bag rested on the rack at the foot of the bed. Someone had already unpacked for her, but her few bits and pieces seemed lonely in the tiny wardrobe. She shook her head to clear away the maze. This is my wedding night, she told herself fiercely.

Her wristwatch warned that time was fleeting. Eight o'clock in the main dining room, Mr Corey had told her. And it was already ten to seven. She skinned out of her clothes, being particularly careful with the dress. A hot bath to relax her, to prepare for the night to come, that's what she needed.

She soaked until the water turned cool. She stepped out of the bath, still agitated. Her hands shook as she slipped on her underthings – black silk briefs, a black camisole top, and the only bright-coloured A-line dress she owned. It was a light summer thing, but surely good enough for an indoor family dinner?

It took a little longer to dry her hair. She left it hanging free down her back. 'But I'll put it up tonight,' she promised herself. One of her girlfriends had told her about that. 'Men will tell you to leave your hair down,' she had said. 'They like to see it all spread across the pillows. And then they go to sleep and roll over on top of it. The first thing *you* know you can't move your

head without being scalped bald!' And that, Penny
Harris, is all you know about getting married, yet here
you are!

Frank had not shown, but it was time to go to
dinner. She snatched up a shawl, just in case it might be
cool in the dining room, and hurried along. The whole
family was waiting for her in the Webster Room.
Except for Frank. They clustered to greet her again.
Kisses were exchanged, and a long happy hug from
Abby.

'But where's Frank?' his mother asked. 'You two
haven't been up to something in the bedroom, have
you?' It was a sly dig, meant to be humorous. Everyone
laughed except Penny. The laughter quickly faded
away.

'I don't know,' she sighed. 'I haven't seen Frank since
the wedding ceremony.' She did her best, but the misery
was set deeply in her tone, and could not be hidden
away.

'Why that—that jackass,' his mother stated. And
then, more softly to her husband, hoping that Penny
would not overhear. 'What in the world is the matter
with the boy?'

'Forty million dollars' worth of pride,' his father
returned, equally softly. But Penny had exceptional
hearing. She slumped down into the proffered chair and
rested both forearms on the table. Abby was seated
beside her.

'You're not mad at Daddy so soon?' the child asked.

'Me? Of course not.' Penny did her best to work up a
smile. 'He's probably very busy at something, love. You
know that we've hurried him unmercifully this week!'

'Probably,' the child responded, dipping into her
chowder.

There was conversation with the meal. The Corey
family was obviously an outgoing group. A bit of
serious discussion was offset by a considerable amount
of teasing, with college-student Ethel bearing the brunt
of it. Halfway through the main course, poached

salmon, Frank arrived. He made no excuses, consulted with nobody, and took a chair at the opposite end of the table from Penny. His arrival shocked her. He looked haggard, worn. His normally immaculate suit was wrinkled, and his tie hung halfway down his shirt.

Penny stared at him, but he avoided her gaze. Well now, she told herself, here's where some experience might help. I don't know what to do! She made a half-hearted attempt to rise, but her mother-in-law, on her left, put a hand on her shoulder in a warning gesture.

The meal ended early. Abby was yawning into her ice cream dish, 'and we have a long trip before us,' Mrs Corey said. 'We have a chartered flight scheduled from Hyannis airport. My husband wants us all to evacuate the area. I don't want you to think our family is terribly important, but a gathering like this so far from home is bound to get some attention in legal circles. And I'm given to understand that attention isn't wanted.'

'I see, but I don't understand,' Penny returned. 'And Frank and I?'

'Why, I expect that you'll stay right here,' Mrs Corey said. 'What better place for a honeymoon? Michael and the other boys are leaving for Boston tonight.'

'And when all the excitement is over we expect you'll join us in Northampton,' she continued. 'Until you find a home of your own, you can all live with us.'

'That will be nice, Gran,' Abby chipped in. 'Are we going now?' There was a general movement from the table. Penny remained in her seat until the confusion of farewells had cleared, then got up and walked around to Frank. He made no move, but she leaned over the back of his chair and put her arms around his chest. Goodbyes were said, she was kissed more times than she had ever been in her life, and then they all were gone, leaving her alone in the room with her husband. Alone, with the exception of three waiters who were hurrying to clear the table. Frank still had not said a word to her. There was a smell of alcohol about him.

Take the bull by the horns, she told herself. I wish I

knew more clichés. I never thought him to be a big
silent type, but if he wants to act coldly, I suppose I
have to put up with it. 'I'm going to bed, Frank.' She
kissed his cheek.

'Yes,' he said, 'why don't you do that?'

Which wasn't much of a send-off for a girl on her
wedding night, she thought as she strolled slowly
around her own ground-floor room. Nothing had
changed. Her few pieces were still the only occupants of
the wardrobe. There was no masculine accumulation in
the bathroom, and very suddenly she was struck by an
ugly premonition. Suppose things *weren't* all right?
Suppose that Frank still had not finished his local job,
whatever that was, and had something more dangerous
to deal with in the night than a lonely bride?

The fun had gone out of everything. Slowly she
prepared for bed. A quick shower, using a cap to keep
her hair dry, a long brushing session, a wondering
selection – the only nightgown she owned that would fit
the circumstances. A pink silk thing, semi-transparent,
cut low in the bodice almost to her waist, and swinging
in a silky slinky fashion around her ankles. She put it
on slowly, hoping to hurry the time, but nothing
happened. She could faintly hear singing and a band
from the Heritage room, across the open courtyard
from her, but not a sound in the halls. And why should
there be? she asked herself. It's only nine-thirty. The
world has a lot of night left to live. 'I'm the only one
going to bed!' And so she did.

The sheets were cool and soft to her touch. After ten
minutes of staring at the ceiling she turned to the
bedside table and picked up one of the paperbacks. The
story was dull, the night quiet. In some deep distance
she heard a clock strike twelve, and then one. The book
slipped from her hands and fell to the floor. The light
glared on, but Penny Harris Corey had fallen into the
darkness.

She awoke at eight. There was a flight of sparrows
disputing rights of way in the courtyard, and the world

was bustling again. Her bleary eyes searched the room. No change. The other half of her bed was still pristinely neat. He had not come. She edged herself up on her pillows and put her hands behind her head, her favourite thinking posture. Something was definitely wrong. Frank?

She was up, scrambling into jeans and a sweater, dashing water into her face, fumbling for shoes. She ran down the corridor into the lobby, down the few stairs to the Conservatory. Frank was sitting at a small table, enjoying his breakfast. He stood up as she approached, and held her chair.

'Did you sleep well?' he asked, heartily cheerful.

'No, I didn't,' she snapped. 'I was up most of the night.'

'Why?' He really didn't seem interested. He was buttering another piece of toast as he asked.

'Because I was waiting for you,' she hissed at him, mindful of the other two couples at breakfast. He put down his knife, arranged it very neatly next to the other silverware, and looked at her. That grim look was on his face again. His eyes were steely cold. 'That was foolish of you,' he said. 'We married so you could claim your forty million dollars, remember?'

'Is that the *only* reason?' She was close to crying, but fought it off. I'm not going to let him make me cry, she told herself. I'm not!

'Well, it seemed big enough at the time,' he said. There was no change in that stern face, not a crack. Not a movement to indicate there was anything more between them than what he had already said.

'Do you really mean that, Frank?' I'm getting to be a great actress, she thought. He doesn't even know I'm crying inside!

'Why, of course I do,' he returned. There was a nervous tic working at the corner of his left eye. At least he's got *some* feeling, she thought. I wonder what it is? Hatred? Does he hate me for trapping him into marriage like this? But *he* asked *me*. Or did his father talk him into it? Well, if the Coreys can play that kind of a game, so can the Harrises. I didn't need him before, and I don't need him now!

'There are ten days until the fifteenth,' she said softly. 'What did you plan to do until then?'

'Oh, I expect to stay around and go with you to Boston,' he said coldly. 'In the meantime, I suppose you might look around the Cape for a while, see the sights, that sort of thing.'

'Tourists,' she snapped. 'You forget that I've lived here for a year, almost.'

'I know.' And the tiredness broke through. 'Can I order you any breakfast?'

'Don't bother,' she snarled. 'I couldn't bear to—I couldn't.' She swallowed hard and pushed her chair back.

'You're leaving?' he asked. 'I thought we might drive down to Provincetown and see the sights.'

'Is that what you really like, Frank?' she snarled. 'P-town is the centre of all the gay life in Massachusetts, you know.'

'What the hell do you mean by that?' he roared, but before he could disentangle himself from the chair and napkin she was gone, fleeing down the hall as if the hounds of hell were after her. Safely back in her room, with the door locked securely behind her, she snatched up her suitcase, threw it on the bed, and began to cram her clothes into it. Not more than five minutes later there came a terrific pounding on the door. 'Penny!' The door rocked on its hinges. 'I know you're in there, Penny. Open the door!'

'Not on your life,' she muttered to herself. The thundering went on for another five minutes before he gave up. She waited a time longer, until she was sure he was gone, then hastily finished her packing. A quick call to the desk brought the promise of an immediate cab. She picked up her suitcase and opened the door cautiously.

The corridor was empty. Instead of going back

through the lobby she went out through the door at the end of the Jarves wing, and looked down towards the portico. A Yellow cab was already there. She ran for it, her bag bouncing off her legs. The driver, who had been watching the lobby, turned around in surprise as she banged into the back seat. 'Please,' she pleaded, 'get me away from here. Barnstable.'

'Town or County?' he asked. A native of the Cape, he was not about to be hurried.

'The town,' she shuddered. 'Do you know Navigation Lane?'

'Yup.'

'Take me there,' she begged. 'Quickly. Oh lord no, I have to stop at the Co-operative Bank.' The word 'bank' seemed to intrigue him. He shifted into gear and roared out of the drive. She watched out the back window as they went, but nobody was chasing her.

It took but a moment to deposit the cheque which her father-in-law had given her, and to get a little cash. Still feeling pursued, she ran back out to the cab and repeated her address. The driver, convinced he had a madwoman on his hands, drove as fast as the law and his elderly cab would allow, dropped her in front of her door, and was off again almost before she could pay him.

There was no sense to being noble now. There was nobody around to see. The tears began slowly, and then cascaded until she was almost blinded by them. She fumbled the key into the front door and headed for the kitchen. It took four trips before she finished loading all the canned goods and the non-perishables into the van. Then she stumbled upstairs and pulled out her camping equipment. The van was crowded by now, but there was still room to spread a sleeping bag and an air mattress. She climbed into the driver's seat, said a short prayer for the motor, and turned on the key. First time lucky. It started immediately. She gave it no time to warm up, but sent the vehicle staggering back up to the highway, turned right on Meetinghouse Way, and followed the old road to the Midcape superhighway.

She stopped at the first rest area going west and pulled out her Woodalls guide to camping areas. Her fingers traced page after page, only to find that most of the sites closed after Labour Day, in September. It was not until she reached the name Rochester that she found what she was looking for—a KOA campground open until November 18th. In an hour, following the directions carefully, she pulled into the wooded family campground and rented a space. 'And now let him find me,' she muttered defiantly as she pitched the tent-adjunct that added valuable space to her little nest. Now let him try to find me! I wonder if he's really looking?

She made a lunch out of tins, using the little butane stove with which the van was equipped, and went for a long walk through the camp, exploring everything. Back to the van by dusk, she managed a sandwich, walked down to the camp shower for a quick cleanup, and was back in her hideaway by eight. The night was dark, overcast. A few lonely stars winked at her and were gone, swallowed up by the cavern of the night. Might as well go to bed, she told herself, and did so.

But going to bed early might have been a terrible mistake. The sounds of the forest night, the hum of far-off motor traffic, did not quite lull her to sleep. Instead it induced cat-naps, each cluttered with scenes she wanted to forget. My wedding, she laughed wryly. What a glorious thing; all virginal white, with flowers. For what? I wonder he even bothered to come. Why couldn't he hire a stand-in as they did in the old days? At least that way I wouldn't have come away with silly ideas—like that he was in love with me. What a laugh that is! By the time she tossed and turned herself to sleep, it was long past midnight, and the threatening storm had broken.

The days passed slowly. The season was long spent, except for the hardiest of campers. But the little lake was pleasant, and she had plenty of wet-weather gear. The nearest other campers were a family of five, about six spaces down from her. When the sun broke out and the children poured out to make up for their enforced confinement, she found herself watching them hungrily, understanding for the first time in her life why some women are tempted to kidnap other people's children.

In no way was it all pleasant, although that was exactly what she told the young manager of the camp at noontime on the fourteenth. She had gotten up early, policed up her campsite, re-packed the van, and stalled around. A salmon sandwich emptied the larder, and she started back up the highway bound for Sandwich, and the Inn. Crossing the canal that separated the real Cape from the rest of Massachusetts, she found herself slipping into the dismals. The old Sagamore bridge, built in the 1930s by the WPA, was now guarded for its entire length by an anti-suicide fence, a steel wire barrier some ten feet high with an inward curve to its top.

She noticed it—not because she was feeling suicidal—but because every mile she drove took her closer to Frank. And every mile cranked up her anger just that one more little notch until, when she took the first exit after the bridge, the one that made a circle under the buttresses of the bridge itself, she was fuming. Another half-hour later she drove into the side parking lot of the Inn, cut her engine and stalked in through the side door. The desk clerk hardly recognised her, but when she gave her name he looked up, startled. 'Mrs Corey?' he asked.

The last name surprised her. It took a moment to adjust. 'Yes,' she admitted. 'Mrs Frank Corey.' The clerk dived for the telephone. 'Your husband is looking for you,' he said as he dialled a number. 'He's almost out of his mind.'

'He's been that way for some years,' she answered coldly. 'Do I still have Room Twenty?'

'And the State Police,' the clerk continued. 'He's got every law outfit on the Cape out looking for you!'

She was too tired to be excited. 'So now they don't have to look any more,' she sighed. 'Do I still have

Room Twenty?'

'They even called out the Air and Sea rescue service,' the clerk babbled on. 'Can you imagine that? The whole Coast Guard station. They thought you might have got lost in the Marshes.'

'That's ridiculous,' she snorted. 'I know the Great Marsh like the back of my hand. Do I still have Room Twenty?'

'And they've had every radio station on the Cape carrying announcements! You should have heard them!'

'Yes, I'll bet it was all terribly exciting,' she yawned. 'I'm tired.'

'You still have Room Twenty, Mrs Corey. Your husband said we should hold it for you until—well, for as long as it took.'

'Do I really?' she said. 'In that case, if I may have my key, I think I'll go and lie down. Do you suppose the porter could bring in my bag? It's out in the old van by the side portico.'

One could. He did. The room hadn't changed an iota since she had walked out, she noticed. Her skin itched. Camping was fine, but there was something about a bath that no camp shower could equal. She filled the bath to its steaming top, was liberal again with somebody else's bubble bath, and sank blissfully down into the warmth. She must have dozed off, because when her room door smashed back with a tremendous crash she started, and noticed that the water was cold.

'Penny! Where the hell are you, girl!' He stomped into the bathroom, glaring. 'Where the hell have you been!' he roared at her. She sank down in the tub, beneath the screening layer of soap bubbles.

'Thank you,' she sighed, 'and I hope you're well too?'

'My God, woman, you've had me tied in knots for a week,' he shouted. 'Not to mention half the police forces on the Cape.'

'How come it took you so long to get worried?' she asked sweetly.

He came over to the side of the tub and kneeled

down. 'And what the hell is that supposed to mean?' he asked.

'You said you'd been worried for a week,' she returned primly, 'and actually I've been gone ten days. Did it take you a few days to discover that you had misplaced one of your possessions?'

'Don't, for God's sake, give me any of that sassy chatter,' he grumbled. 'I don't need that!'

'Maybe you do,' she returned. 'Maybe there are just too many people in the world who jump every time you snap your fingers. Well, I'm not one of them, Frank Corey. And as to where I've been, that's my business. I promised your father I'd meet him here on the night of the fourteenth, and here I am. I don't remember making any promise to you—in fact it seems to me you were more than glad to see the back of me. Now, if we've settled all this satisfactorily, would you mind leaving my bathroom? I'd like to get out of this bath before I freeze to death.'

'I'll get you out,' he snapped, 'and no, we haven't finished this little conversation yet, believe me.'

'Oh, I believe you,' she snarled, 'but I *have* finished the conversation. I don't believe I've got a single thing to talk to you about. Not a single—what are you doing?' He was wearing a coat and tie, a very expensive-looking coat, but without hesitation he shoved his arms down into the tub, under the soap, under her, and whirled her up out of the bath as if she were a featherweight.

'Put me down,' she roared at him. 'You—you lecher! Put me down!' She almost made her escape. Soaking wet, splattered liberally with soap, she was as slippery as a seal. But he managed to keep a hold on her by squeezing her up against his beautiful ruffled shirt. She added a few kicks for effect, then tried to box his ears with both hands. Before she could do him damage he managed to get her out to the bedroom, where he dropped her, still dripping wet, on the bed. 'Now look what you've done,' she moaned. 'You've ruined a perfectly good bed!'

'I'll ruin considerably more than that before this night is over,' he threatened. He stomped back into the bathroom, seized a couple of towels, and came back again, throwing both of them at her. The edge of her anger was wearing off, replaced by fear. She was a big girl; he was a bigger man. And it wasn't 'love and for ever after' that sparkled in his eyes. It was more like 'Jack the Ripper Finds True Love!' She shrank back on the bed, suddenly aware of her own nudity. She mustered the towels into a protective front. But he was having no part of that.

He sat down on the bed beside her, still glaring. 'My father is already waiting for us,' he said. His voice was lower, but no less menacing. 'He's gone through all kinds of gyrations for you, and damn you, you're going to be there. You hear me?'

'I'm not afraid of him because he's got a big voice,' she told herself. And he'd better not get tough with me. I didn't take all those karate lessons for nothing. But he was a dirty fighter. Instead of taking a good honest swing at her jaw, he picked up one of the towels and began to dry her off, starting at her toes and slowly working his way upward. And all the while his eyes were touring the rest of her, left on plain view by her sudden paralysis. By the time he got to her knees she began to bless the fact that she was already lying down, for surely her knees would not have been able to hold her up.

When he came further north, up the incline of her thighs, she could feel all of her anger easing out of her, being replaced by an excitement she had not felt before. It felt so strange that she opened an eye and looked. He had lost the towel, and didn't seem to realise it. Or maybe he did. It took a great deal of strength, but she managed to pull herself out of her daze. She grabbed the other towel and pushed it down into his hands. His head came up in surprise. Either he had forgotten the towel, she thought, or he's just had too much experience with women!

'Think!' she muttered. 'You don't want me! You've already shown me that more than once.' It was hard to keep the bitterness from showing. He leaned back on his heels and very slowly pulled his hands off her. She snatched at both towels, using one to cover her dripping breasts, leaving the other draped across her hips.

'A lot you know,' he returned. 'Any old port in a storm. Maybe I *do* want you.' He stood up and took off his coat and shirt. She huddled back in the bed, her mind a complete blank. He's my husband, her conscience told her. He has rights. But not like this. Not like this!

He sat down on the bed again and began to pull off his shoes and socks. It mut have been then that he noticed the fear, the deep shock in her eyes. 'Now what are you thinking?' he asked wryly. 'Has it finally come to your attention that your husband might want to rape you?'

She mustered up the last of her bravado. 'Well, if that's what you're going to do, please get it over quickly. I've got to get some sleep tonight!'

'Damn you!' he groaned. One sweep of his hand dislodged the towel over her breasts, sending it spinning into the corner. 'It wouldn't take much, would it?'

'How would I know?' she stuttered, as one of his hands stroked her midriff, then slid up to her breast, 'I've never tried it before, have I?'

'How would I know?' he returned. His hand was climbing the mountain, sending signals which she had never received before. Sending messages that needed no interpretation. And she didn't want him to stop, but stop he did. With both her nipples straining upward, her hips moving uneasily, her face crossed by passions she had never known, he stopped.

'What do you know,' he laughed. 'All I wanted to do was to take off my wet clothes. Rape is not on the cards tonight, little lady. Are you really a virgin?'

'That's something you'll never find out,' she snarled at him, humiliated more than she could tell. Whoever called it a fate worse than death must have been a man, she told herself. The first chance I get I'm going to kick him right where it will hurt! She started to roll off the bed. His hands seized on her arms and locked her in position.

'No you don't,' he laughed. 'I don't intend to have you maim me—at least not tonight!' Neither of them heard the light knock on the door, repeated twice. Neither noticed the turn of the knob. They both were staring deep into each other's eyes, she completely naked, he half so, when his father stuck his head around the door jamb.

'I thought you had both got lost,' the older Mr Corey laughed. 'So I thought I'd better come down and speed you—ooops! Excuse me!' The door slammed behind him. 'Come when you're ready,' he yelled from the corridor. Frank released Penny's arms and she slid off the bed, holding one of the towels in a strategic position. He got up too, picked up his wet things, and made for the door.

'I'm two doors down,' he said. 'Knock when you're ready to go.'

She went to the door behind him, closed it between them, and leaned against the strength of it. For a girl who doesn't cry in public, Penny Corey, she told herself, you sure do a lot of it in private!

CHAPTER NINE

SHE was up before the birds. The sun had not yet cleared the horizon, but the sky was cloudless, with a tiny breeze boxing the compass. Running through her mind was the recurrent theme: this is the day. This is the day! She went through her necessary morning drill, remembering her father-in-law's admonition. 'Dress nearly, demurely,' he had laughed over the dinner table the night before. 'Look as if butter wouldn't melt in your mouth!' The only rag she owned that met the description was her wedding dress. She fondled it lovingly before slipping it on, and spent minutes smoothing it down, checking it out. The low heels again. Frank was coming with them, and in his present mood she had no intention of giving him something to pick on.

It had been a quiet dinner. Frank had come out as soon as she had knocked on his door, grasping her arm with talons that left marks, hurrying her along to the dinner-table without saying a word. His father had been somewhat more pleasant, but even he was busy with last-minute papers. 'Including a sheriff's deputy,' he said. 'With forty million dollars at stake you just never know what might happen.' She flashed a quick look at Frank. As soon as the money was mentioned his face went cold, and he looked away from her.

Abby had not exactly helped, either. During the dessert course a waiter came in with a telephone, plugged it in, and handed it to her. 'Mama,' the little voice said, 'when are you coming home?'

'Abby!' Penny was startled. In her group people made long-distance calls only when somebody has won the lottery, or when a member of the family died! 'How did you get through to me?'

139

'Why—' That wasn't exactly what the child wanted to talk about, and it took her a minute or two to catch up to the question. 'But all you gotta do is dial the numbers. Gran marked them down on the telephone pad and I just dialled them!' Which left Penny without a rock to stand on. Direct-distance dialling. Leave your four-year-old alone in the room with a telephone, and the next month's bill will include two calls to London! 'Mama,' the child repeated, 'when are you coming home?'

'I don't know,' she said softly, trying to avoid the curious eyes that surrounded her. 'I just don't know. It depends on what your grandfather does, and what your father says. Are you all right, darling?'

'No, my tooth hurts, and I'm lonesome. You gotta come home quick, Mama.'

'I'll do what I can, love,' she answered. 'Do you want to speak to your father?'

'Nope. I just wanna talk to you. Somebody's coming.' The telephone crashed down at the far end, leaving Penny in no doubt that the call had been unauthorised. She set the receiver down carefully, and tried to look innocent as she looked around the table.

'Nothing important,' she said, and glued her lips together, determined to say not another word. And so that was the way it had been. On an emotional high at one minute, and down the next, like a crazy roller-coaster ride that left her completely drained. And now, on this important morning, things were the same. An emotional high as she dressed, even to the point of singing to herself as she opened the door to a light knock. Frank, again with that cold hard face. Her spirits plummeted. He walked her through the lobby to the front portico, and then she took hold of herself. I am not, she promised herself, going to let *that man* ruin my day. *I am not!*

She worked up a smile, and switched to her father-in-law's arm. Frank seemed taken aback. His father smiled broadly, gave her hand a little pat, and tucked it securely in the crook of his arm.

The car that was waiting for them was enough to take her breath away. One of those special stretched-out limousines, it was ten feet longer than a normal car, and looked like a great grey shark, just waiting to do something drastic. 'Wow!' was all Penny could think to say, and it shamed her. All those years in school, under her grandfather's tutelage, and all she could muster was 'Wow!'

'From here on,' Mr Corey explained, 'we do everything first class. Where the devil is that mink coat I asked Edith to send down? Didn't you get it?'

'I—she did send it,' Penny sighed, 'but I just couldn't wear it. All those poor animals, just so I could swank it up.'

'I could have wished you to start the day off a little harder in the heart,' her lawyer laughed. 'And don't get carried away by all this front we're putting up. The limo is rented.'

'Oh, that's a break,' she giggled.

'Don't laugh too hard,' her husband gloomed. 'It'll be on the bill.'

'You'll be with me, Frank, so I won't be too—scared?' She reached for his hand.

'That's not on the programme,' his father chuckled. 'We're going in to play a little penny-ante with these people. If we brought Frank into the conference, the way he's been this week, it would be Custer's Last Stand instead. No sir, Penelope, you and your lawyer will play this scene by ourselves. Frank can sit out in the lobby or something. I don't think it will take long. All the paperwork is complete.'

'I—I don't think I'd like being there very long,' Penny mumbled. 'Uncle Henry will be there. And Oscar, and all the nephews. I don't think I'm going to like it at all without Frank being there!'

'Who the devil is Oscar?' her husband demanded.

She looked at him in surprise. 'I didn't tell you about Oscar? I thought I did. He's my—third cousin, or something. Uncle Henry plans for me to marry Oscar.

I'll tell you something. Uncle Henry worries me; Oscar scares me.' She huddled down in her seat, depressed by the thought.

'Don't let it frighten you,' Frank said. 'You're too much of a romantic for this hard cold life, Penny. You keep thinking that my father is Sir Galahad, and righteousness will triumph. It doesn't work that way. Think of yourself as going in there in the company of a Great White Shark, who's going to glide around and bite the hell out of them when they're not looking. I'll be glad to wait outside. You don't need me to settle your damn forty million dollars.' And that was his last word.

Penny's heart settled just a little lower than the straps on her very practical flat-heeled shoes. Lord, she told herself bitterly, I thought he might be upset by a hundred of my bad habits; instead he's going wild at me because I inherited all that money! If this scheme doesn't work today, I'm a cooked goose! She looked over at her father-in-law with a special pleading in her eyes. He smiled, winked, and handed her a couple of papers.

'Learn your lines,' he said. 'Most people aren't as smart as you think they are. There's a large difference between *smart* and *clever*. I get the impression that your uncle is pretty clever. Unfortunately for him, by the time we sit down at the table the case will be all sewn up. By the way, the meeting is scheduled downtown in the financial district. Maybe you'd like to stop by your house and freshen up?'

She shuddered, and moved over in the seat to squeeze closer to Frank. 'If you mean the house in Gainsborough Street,' she said, 'I don't ever want to go into that house again. That was Grandfather's house—and now it's where Uncle Henry lives. I—I just don't have the guts for that. No.'

'Good,' her father-in-law chuckled. 'Shall we throw that on the pile too?'

'Yes. Yes, please. I actually forgot about that!' He made a note on the side of one of his long yellow pads.

'And that,' he concluded, screwing the top back on to his gold pen, 'will take care of everything. Hey, look at this!' They had, after an hour of steady driving, arrived in Winthrop Square, in the financial heart of Boston. The red-brick structure before them had been built old and solid, and then newly refurbished within the decade. 'For a charitable Foundation, this thing looks as if they believe in the old adage about charity beginning at home,' her father-in-law chuckled. 'Is anybody looking?'

'There were three people in the fourth-floor window,' Frank reported. 'They've ducked out of sight. They saw us all right.'

'That's what we needed,' his father replied. 'There's no sense to all this conspicuous consumption if nobody sees us arrive. If Cinderella had arranged for a few witnesses she wouldn't have had all the trouble she did. Will you just look at that building? I'll bet it costs more to rent per square foot than my puny little Hershoff yacht! Well, the meeting is scheduled for fifteen minutes from now. It gives the opposition time to worry a little bit about what we're up to.'

'Do they—does Uncle Henry know we're coming?' Penny asked.

'He knows someone is coming,' her lawyer told her. 'The bank notified them that a representative would be present.'

'A representative?'

'Surely. Me. Where the devil is that doctor we're supposed to meet?'

Too confused to remain quiet, Frank tried to stick an oar in. 'What doctor?' he asked. His father looked at him and grinned.

'I thought you weren't interested in any of this,' he observed, 'so suffer. Is that him, Penny? Or rather them?'

Three men stepped out of the lobby of the building and walked smartly over to the car. The hired chauffeur opened one of the rear doors and they crowded into the car. The elder of the three, grey-haired, grey-topcoated against the wind, offered a hand.

'Doctor Ketelman,' he introduced himself. 'And our senior accountants, Mr Jimson and Mr Hall. Are you sure this isn't all a dream, Mr Corey?'

'I couldn't be more right, Doctor. This is the little lady in question, my daughter-in-law, Penelope Harris Corey.'

'She's not anybody's *little lady*,' Frank grumbled. 'She's my wife!' And look how long it's taken you to make up your mind about *that*, Penny thought. Do you really mean it, or am I becoming a bone for a couple of dogs to fight over? It was just too hard to accept that he meant what he said, not after her long terrible wedding day, and the ten days that had followed!

The doctor looked Frank over carefully, then reached up and snapped on the interior lights. 'Dyspeptic is what they called it when I first started to practice medicine, young man. Not enough sleep, too much tension. You need to relax. Let me take your pulse.'

'Dammit!' Frank roared. 'That's the ever-loving end.' He snatched his hand out of the doctor's clutch, banged the door open, and went stalking down the block.

'Oh dear,' Penny sighed. All her confidence had just oozed out the door, and was being blown away in circles by the whirling wind. Her father-in-law's hand came over to cover hers. He picked up the conversation as if Frank had not been there.

'And the Institute has no objections,' he continued to the doctor.

'Objections! My dear sir, the roof of the place must have gone up two feet when I explained it all to the Board. And no more than just in time, it was. We had a terrible fire last night. The trailer that houses all our office equipment was completely destroyed. We live from day to day, you know, and this looks like the first month in heaven to us!'

'If it will make you feel any better,' Mr Corey chuckled, 'the little lady has just added a three-storey brownstone over on Gainsborough Street. It would make a nice office building, although I suspect you'd want to see for yourself. They are all being converted to condominiums over there. It should go—oh—another half a million.'

'Oh dear!' the doctor said.

'Oh dear,' Penny sighed. She had missed all the byplay, watching Frank. He disappeared around the far corner. Suppose he did that and never came back? She could feel the shivers mounting in her soul.

'He's only gone to walk it off,' Mr Corey said. 'It's a habit he picked up when he came back from Vietnam. He'll walk a few blocks, and things will settle down. You'll see.' He patted her hand and leaned closer. 'You know, don't you, love, that a good many of our brightest young men came back from that war troubled? Frank had more than his share. You have to make allowances.'

'Yes, I know,' she replied. Her emotions had just hit a new low, and she wanted nothing more than to turn back the clock, to go back to the Cape and wipe everything out of her mind. Her lawyer squeezed her hand. 'You're a good woman, Penelope,' he said. 'Maybe too good for my son. Come now, it's time to go.'

She demanded a moment or two in the lobby while she shed her plain cloth coat and did her best to rearrange her dress. 'Something simple,' her father-in-law had told her the night before. 'Dignified, but simple. They expect a pliable little thing who'll snap to when they crack the whip!' And here she was in her wedding dress, feeling just as out of place here as when she had first worn it. She had left her hair loose. It seemed to reduce her age by a decade.

'You look fine,' Mr Corey told her. 'You look fine.' His hand gently rearranged the little gold cross she wore on a thin gold chain, her only jewellery. 'Here we go!'

The lift delivered them to the fourth floor with a

great deal of dignity, but not much speed. It disgorged them into a plant-filled anteroom where a smiling little blonde receptionist looked up at them from behind a modernistic desk.

'There is a meeting of the Board of Directors,' Mr Corey stated. Everything about him had changed. His voice shifted to a deeper bass; all the glittering fun had gone out of it. It sounded like something that Moses might have heard on the mountain. The thought tickled Penny's fancy. She took his arm and was actually smiling as they followed the blonde down the corridor.

'I'm afraid the meeting has already begun,' the girl said, switching her wad of gum from one cheek to the other. 'I don't think I can let you interrupt them at this time.'

'I don't think you have a great deal of choice,' Mr Corey laughed as he set her aside. There was a very large well-formed young man waiting by the door. As their party came up, he reached into his pocket and pinned on a badge.

'Mr Corey?' he asked. 'Sergeant Mills. The Commander said I was to come and lend a hand.'

'What exactly were your instructions?'

The young man hesitated, then, 'The Commander said I was to come and give you a hand in anything except rape and murder. I think maybe that was just an expression, you know.'

'I know,' Mr Corey chuckled. 'The Commander and I went to law school together. We go a long way back. And there, what did I tell you, Penny?' She looked furtively behind her. Frank was stalking up the corridor. 'I'll wait here,' he said, pulling a lightweight plastic chair over by one of the windows. His father nodded. 'Gentlemen,' he said. He reached for the knobs of the double doors, and threw them both open. 'Me first,' he told Penny as he sauntered into the room.

She had seen this room only once before. Years ago she had come here hesitantly to ask Uncle Henry for some pin-money. Her grandfather had run the entire

business out of his hat. Her uncle required a
Boardroom a good fifty feet long, with a massive oak
table, in addition to his desk. Six men sat at that table
now. She knew them all. Her uncle occupied the head
chair, managing to look remarkably like the father of
the Wicked Witch of Oz. Cousin Oscar sat at his right
hand, a huge bulking man who looked like a free-
standing oil drum, even when wearing a new suit, as he
was at the moment. The other four were nonentities,
nephews of her uncle but no real relatives of her own.
The argument which had been going on stopped in mid-
sentence as everyone at the table turned around to look
at them.

Penny had been walking in Mr Corey's shadow, but
now moved to one side to see what was going on.
'You!' her uncle roared. 'I knew it had to be something
like this. So you're at the bottom of it all, are you? Do
you think we've nothing better to do than sit around
waiting for the likes of you to show up? Get over here
and sign these proxies, and then you can go back to
your dolls!'

Her hands were shaking. She tucked one of them
under her father-in-law's elbow. I'm not scared, she told
herself. I'm not! Frank is—out there watching over me,
and I'm not scared! I'm just so—so angry I could spit.
Look at Oscar grinning at me, like a bear looking for a
place to bite! Wait until Papa gets at him. Papa! That's
what everyone else called Mr Corey, and he had
suggested in the car that she do the same. She went up
on tiptoes and whispered in his ear, 'The smiling one is
Oscar, the cousin they all want me to marry.'

Her father-in-law gave her a big smile and gestured
her to the table. Instead of marching around the table
smartly to sign the proxies that would allow her uncle
to cast *her* vote, she took the chair at the bottom of the
table, carefully arranged her purse and notes in front of
her, and smiled brightly at them all.

'I'm glad to see you all in good health,' she said.
There was a lilt in her voice that none of them had ever

heard before. The demure little girl sat there in front of them, but somebody else was inside that beautiful head of hers.

'You must excuse me,' she continued. 'I've been out of society for a long time and have forgotten my manners. May I present Mr Michael Corey, my lawyer.'

A cloud of gloom seemed to have gathered around the room. 'You don't need a lawyer,' her uncle shouted at her, 'you need your head examined!' It was just the sort of approach he had always used, brow-beating the child into submission. But the child had changed.

'You're right as always, Uncle Henry,' she said. 'I *do* need my head looked at. May I also present my doctor, Dr Ketelman.' Mr Corey gave them all a big smile as he pulled out the chair next to Penny. She watched as he carefully opened his briefcase and began to line up little piles of paper in front of him. Look at that, Penny thought. Just as Frank said. He's a monster shark, getting ready to bite somebody. Lord, I'm glad he's on my side!

The doctor took up a chair on her other side. The other two men in her party joined them. Her cousins were looking more puzzled than persuaded. 'And these two gentlemen are my accountants,' she concluded.

It was almost as if she had thrown a bomb at them. They all blanched. Her uncle pushed his chair back, started to get up and then thought better of it. 'They have no right being here,' he roared.

'Ah!' Her father-in-law got up, lazily spreading the papers a little wider apart, like a set of playing cards. 'And who is the Secretary of the Board?' The young man closest to them—Penny remembered that his name was Bob something or other—raised his hand. Far more than Uncle Henry, Bob looked harassed, a weasel look on his face.

'Now then,' Mr Corey continued. He flicked through the papers in front of him, picked one out, and skidded it down the table to the Secretary. 'The last Will and

Testament of Philip J. Harris,' he said. 'This copy comes from the Court of Probate, and is sealed by the clerk of the Court. Page four, paragraph six, and I quote, "And upon the twenty-first birthday of my granddaughter, Penelope Harris, or her marriage, all said shares in the possession of the Bank of Boston are to be turned over to said granddaughter to be used in any way she may see fit. It is my further desire that she then assume automatic membership on the Board of Directors of the Foundation, without further vote.'

'How the hell did you get that?' Uncle Henry turned colours. His nose and forehead were a brilliant red, and it almost seemed as if his cheeks had turned green.

'Strange, isn't it?' Mr Corey grinned. 'There are no real secrets left in the whole wide world. Would you like me to tell you what the Governor had for breakfast this morning?' He flipped up another sheet of paper, and slid it down the table. 'A certificate from the Bank, stating that upon presentation of proper and satisfactory evidence, Penelope Harris has become the owner of record of twenty thousand shares of stock in the Foundation. Each share of stock, of course, is worth one vote. And these——' he held up the bundle of papers '—are the shares themselves. Shall we get on with the day's business?'

'Old business,' Oscar growled. 'A vote to increase the salaries of all directors by twenty-five per cent.'

'That's already approved.' Uncle Henry waved the idea away. 'Get on with it.'

'But a vote is required,' Mr Corey said silkily. Uncle Henry frowned. And it doesn't frighten me one bit, Penny lectured herself. What can he possibly do to me now?

'Vote!' her uncle roared, and banged the table. Six yes votes were heard promptly. Penny took a deep breath and said, 'No.'

'Six to one.' Her uncle thumped the table again. 'The motion is carried.'

'There's a slight problem there,' Mr Corey chuckled.

'Penny has just cast twenty thousand negative votes, against your five thousand affirmative.'

Uncle Henry seemed about to choke. He ripped his necktie loose, sputtered, and banged on the table again. Oscar leaned over and whispered something in his ear. A grim smile flashed over his face. 'The motion is defeated,' he said, 'for the moment. New Business?'

Penny could feel the trembling start all the way down to her toes and work its way up. Her knees seemed to rattle like a car on the Red Line, the old subway. She looked around, but no one else seemed to hear them. She swallowed. 'I am informed by my accountants,' she said softly, 'that certain members of this Board will be indicted by a Grand Jury in the next week for embezzlement. I move that we replace the present Chairman of the Board with——' She stopped to send one last appeal to her father-in-law. He shook his head, leaned over, and whispered, 'This is it, little lady!'

She took a deep breath and stared around the table at them all. With a firm voice she said, 'I move that Penelope Harris be elected chairman of this Board. Vote, please.' The numbers came out the same, and her uncle could see the handwriting on the wall. He stood up and glared at her. For some reason he didn't seem as big as she remembered. He was really just a tired, mean old man.

'We'll settle this when we get home, young lady,' he snapped. He stalked to the door and slammed through it. Outside they could hear his voice raised in anger as the police sergeant detained him. Mr Corey leaned over again. 'Nice going, Madam Chairperson. Now, up to the head of the table, and don't forget your lines. Bang the gavel a lot. That often helps.'

'All by myself?' she whispered. 'I—I can't do that!'

'You can and you will,' he encouraged. 'You swallowed the lion, why gag on the mouse? Right now!'

She struggled to her feet and walked around the table, keeping close to the wall all the way. Her new position put her next to Oscar—and you *are* scared of him, aren't you, little mouse, she asked herself. You don't deserve to be married to a nice man like Frank. Mouse!

She took the Chair, shrinking away from Oscar. The little gavel seemed to weigh ten tons. She banged it gently on the little block of wood provided.

'I now move to——' and she stopped. Everything had slipped out of her mind. She shivered and looked down to the little card cupped in her hand, covered with a spider-web of instructions. 'I now move to order a complete audit of all funds of this Foundation. Vote.' The hammer fell again.

'Cut it out,' Oscar said hoarsely, leaning in her direction. 'It's all just a funny exercise for you, isn't it? Well, it's a waste of time. I've already got our marriage licence in my pocket, and we'll be married tomorrow. You must have thought we were a bunch of dummies, not to be prepared for something like this!'

She looked at him as if seeing him for the first time. Just another bully. Bigger than Uncle Henry, but the same sort of man. She began to giggle. 'Papa,' she called down the length of the table, 'Oscar wants to marry me tomorrow.'

'So what's so funny?' her cousin growled. 'Just knock off the hilarity, Penelope, or you'll get what's coming to you!'

She stifled her giggles and turned a solemn face to him. Her eyes seemed bigger than her head. Her teeth were clenched, but she barely managed to force them open as she lay her left hand out on the table in front of him. 'I'm afraid it won't be convenient for me to marry you tomorrow,' she said softly, 'and besides, my husband might not approve.' She wiggled her third finger, flashing spears of light from the garish ring Frank had given her.

'Your husband!' He kicked his chair back and toppled it over on to the rug. 'Why you bitch! You mean you ran off and married somebody else?'

'I guess that's just what I must have done,' she

sighed. He was big, Oscar was. She had never wanted to fight with him. But it was coming, and right now. She could feel it in the air. 'I never meant to hurt you, Oscar,' she placated, 'but I can't imagine that you were ever in love with me. In fact I don't even think you ever liked me. But—well, that's the way it is. Oh, by the way, my lawyer is also my father-in-law.'

She could see it coming. That big fist, swinging almost as in a slow-motion picture, in a roundhouse right, coming directly at her head. Everything seemed to be moving ever so slowly. Oh no, she thought, not on my head! She jumped up from her chair and started to turn away from him. The blow, with all the malevolence that her cousin could muster behind it, bounced off her shoulder and knocked her across the room. Both her hands came up to shield her face, but the force of the blow hurled her head first squarely at the wall. And all the time she was flying through the air she could hear someone screaming, 'Frank! Frank!'

The double doors at the end of the conference room seemed to bounce off their hinges as he came through. She had hardly slipped to the floor before he was there, snatching her up, pinioning her arms around her head. 'Nothing's happened, really,' she stammered through the pain of it. 'My head. It'll be all right in a minute.'

'Damn your head,' he muttered, 'what the hell happened?'

She waved in the general direction of the table. 'He hit me,' she said softly.

Luckily her hands were still guarding her head, because before she could add a qualifier, Frank had dropped her back on to the rug and was at the conference table. 'This one?' he grated, but paid no attention to her answer. His hands closed on the collar of her youngest cousin Ralph, who had been sitting on her left at the table. Before Ralph could offer a word in his own defence he was lifted straight up off his chair, whirled around once, and bounced down on the carpet as Frank's fist drew blood from his nose.

'That's not the one,' his father yelled from the foot of the table. The older Corey had been caught by surprise, and was only now getting into motion.

'Oh? This one?' Frank was going down the line of nephews like a reaper in a field of ripe wheat. Chairs banged, overturned, but there was no escape from his enraged hands.

'None of those.' His father had finally managed to get his attention. 'That big one over there, that's Oscar.'

'God, I even hate that name,' Frank yelled. He walked back by Penny. She huddled up in the corner. 'You all right?' he asked, but didn't wait for an answer. The battle light still shown in his eyes. His face looked as if it were made of stone. Very slowly he walked back to the head of the table, picking up each of the overturned chairs and returning them to their proper position. Up one side of the table, and around the end.

'You?' His voice was a deadly hiss, the sound of a cobra about to strike. 'You hit my wife?'

Oscar was the type of man for whom statues are dedicated. Big, strong, single-minded and stupid. 'Sure,' he announced, 'I hit the bitch. And as soon as I take care of you I'll do it again.'

Penny blinked her eyes. She didn't want to watch. Her body was reporting various little aches and pains that she hadn't noticed before. Oscar was taller than Frank. Three or four inches taller. And heavier. Twenty or thirty pounds of advantage. So how was it that while she had her eyes closed temporarily, Oscar was sliding down the length of the highly polished table on his stomach, with blood streaming from *his* nose?

Frank dived after him, and they both came off the opposite end of the table, scattering Dr Ketelman and his cohort like a bunch of nine-pins. By the time Oscar had struggled to his feet and made a dash for the doors, Frank was close behind him. They could hear a continued series of thuds in the outer lobby, then everything went quiet. Penny hardly noticed as the remainder of her 'cousins' filtered out of the room, trying to look as unobtrusive as possible.

Her father-in-law came around the table and helped her to her feet. His steady hand guided her wandering feet back to her chair. 'Madam Chairwoman,' he chuckled, 'if your brains aren't too scrambled, it would be a good time to complete the final items on the agenda.'

Twenty minutes later she and Dr Ketelman were alone in the conference room. She signed her name one last time, then gave him the pen to keep. 'That's one of the properties of the Foundation too,' she giggled. For some reason her head ached, her back ached, and her heart ached. When she needed him, Frank had come. How did that equate with his behaviour since the wedding? It was a problem she could not solve.

'We'll have that pen framed and mounted in our main lobby,' the doctor commented. 'You're a brave, thoughtful girl, Penelope. My, that's a big bump you've got on your head. Does it hurt?'

'Only when I move my head,' she answered, 'not very much.'

He looked closely into each of her eyes in turn. 'I suppose there could be some slight concussion,' he noted. 'I take it you're newly married?'

'I—yes, just a few days.'

'Then let me prescribe for you,' he chuckled. 'Go home with that husband of yours, take two aspirins, and go to bed.'

'And then what?'

'He'll think of something. A little light exercise would be nice for you, but stay in bed.'

That was the moment that they walked out through the swinging doors. As a result, the only witness to her wild impulse to kiss the doctor was her husband. And then they were alone.

Frank turned his back on her and sat down in the receptionist's chair. There were plenty of plants around, but not another seat to be had. Her head *did* hurt. She walked around to the front of the desk, papers in one hand, crossed fingers on the other. 'Frank?'

'What?' That gruff tone again that chilled her. She was determined to force the issue now, but he took the lead. 'Did you get your damn forty million dollars settled?'

She fidgeted, not quite knowing what to do next. 'Yes,' she whispered, 'it's all settled. What do we do now?'

He swivelled the chair around to face her. 'Well, you've got what you married me for,' he said, 'and I hope your money will make you happy. Here.' He handed her a little calling card. 'That's the name of a particularly good friend of mine. He's a lawyer too. I've already spoken to him by telephone.'

There was no relaxation in him. He spoke as if he were a million miles away, commenting on the craters of the moon. Penny stiffened her shoulders. Her pride was interfering with her life, she knew, but could not help it; she was that sort of girl.

'And what do you want me to do?' she pressed. The pleading had gone out of her voice. She spoke as coolly as he.

'I would *suggest*,' he said, 'that you go home to Gainsborough Street. It ought to be perfectly safe. They took your Uncle Henry to jail, so he can't bother you. And then I would *suggest* that you see a doctor about your bumps and bruises.'

'And then?'

'And then, when you get yourself under control, I *suggest* that you drop in and see my friend there, Charlie Zimmerman, and he'll take care of things for you.'

'What things?' she demanded.

'Do I have to spell it all out?' He acted as if he were hurt by her lack of comprehension.

'Yes,' she said. 'I'm the kid from the cranberry bog, remember?'

'Then you can get an annulment,' he snapped, and

turned the chair round so she could no longer see his face.

'Is that what you want? Is that really what you want?'

'It's what you need,' he grunted. 'You've got your money. You don't need me any more. There's a cab waiting for you downstairs. It's practically painless, they tell me, getting an annulment. And you can count on me for any testimony you might need.'

'You planned it all the time, didn't you?' she accused him. 'That's why we had a civil ceremony with no fanfare, and no announcements. Yes, I can see things now that bothered me very much before.' She was determined not to cry—not to let him see the effect it was all having on her. 'You're sure, Frank?'

She could see him shrug his shoulders. It was her pride that turned her away from the desk, and pride that pushed the lift button. She held herself stiffly, never looking back, but when the doors closed behind her the silent tears gradually welled up and drained down her cheeks. She could barely see when she reached the main floor. The big limousine was at the kerb, a cab in front of it, meter ticking. Her father-in-law climbed out.

'Where's Frank?' And then he noticed the tears. 'Dear God, what has that fool son of mine done now! Wait here. I'm going back up to talk to him.'

She restrained him by clutching at his coat-cuff. 'No,' she sobbed. 'It's our marriage, *only* ours. Don't interfere. and don't ever tell Frank what I did with the money. Promise?' She didn't want Frank's pity, not now he had made it clear he wanted nothing to do with her.

He looked at her as if making the promise would be difficult. Then he shrugged his shoulders. 'Yes, it's your marriage,' he said. 'And you can count on me to never say a word. Will you come back to Northampton with me?'

She shook her head dumbly. He watched uneasily, as a man does when a woman cries, and then climbed back into the limo. She leaned down over the door before he closed it. 'I—I've come to—love you all,' she stammered. 'Tell Abby—tell——' And the tears came again. She closed the limousine door and walked up to the cab. The cabbie saw her, and opened the rear door.

'Gainsborough Street, the man said?' He started the cab. She looked back towards the building they were leaving. Frank was standing in the fourth-floor window, watching. She waited until he was out of sight, and then tapped on the glass. 'Take me to the bus station,' she sighed through her tears.

CHAPTER TEN

'So,' his mother roared back at him, 'why shouldn't I treat you like that? You walk around like a bear with a sore head and you expect everyone to be sweet to you? The war was over years ago!'

'It's got nothing to do with the war,' Frank roared back at her. And then more softly, considerately, 'I'm sorry, Mom. It's just——'

'We are all aware of what it's just,' his mother interrupted, hearing the pain in his voice. 'You've been a tremendous damn fool, and now you don't know what to do about it. Isn't that right? Well, don't stand around here telling *me* about it, go tell *her*!'

'That's the damn problem,' he sighed. 'Would you believe it, even my own daughter won't speak to me—and I think if I met a guy like me I wouldn't speak to me either. But I can't very well tell her about it.'

'Pride?'

'Pride, hell. I just can't *find* her!'

His mother plumped down in a kitchen chair. She had been baking pies for the holiday, and her flushed cheeks masked the concern she felt for her youngest son. Poor Frank. Poor mangled heart-torn Frank, who had been through so much. 'Where have you looked?' she asked.

'Well, first of all, with Charlie Zimmerman. I gave her his card, and—you wouldn't believe this—I recommended she go to him for an annulment.' He pulled up a chair beside her and sat down. 'I should have my head examined,' he swore softly. 'How could any one man be so damn stupid? I love her so much it hurts, and I told her to go and get an annulment.'

'And she hasn't been to Zimmerman?'

'No. Charlie says he hasn't seen her or heard from

her. Not that she couldn't have gone to some other lawyer, of course. She might have been so—so angry with me that she would call anything black if I said it was white.'

'Did she have good cause to be angry with you?'

'Of course she did. I *said* that. It wasn't her, it was that damn forty million dollars. How in the world could I go around and hold my head up under that? Who would believe I didn't marry her for her money?'

'Yes, I can see that would be a problem. Where else did you look?'

'Well, she has a house in Boston, out on Gainsborough Street. One of those old three-storey brownstones. Victorian—but a fine place. I thought she'd go there. I told her to.'

His mother shook her head. Even the best of men can be so stupid, she thought. He *told* her to get an annulment; he told her to go to this house. What would any spirited girl do? Exactly the opposite, of course!

'And she wasn't there, I take it?'

'Not a bit. *Nobody*'s living there. You know they took her so-called uncle and that Oscar fellow away? They've both been indicted for embezzlement, and the pair of them applied for passports before the initial hearing.'

'What does that mean?'

'I don't know what that means, but the judge took it as *prima facie* evidence that they meant to skip the country, so he ordered them held without bail in the County jail. Well, anyway, I went to the house on Gainsborough Street. Penny wasn't there. Nobody was there, and the neighbours told me that while everything else on the street was going condominium, someone had made an appeal for a zoning variance to make an office building out of it. Some medical group, they said. I didn't pay much attention. All I wanted to know I found out—she isn't there now, she hasn't been there since November the fifteenth—and I don't have any real idea where the hell she is.'

'It must have been a very lonely Christmas for her, Frank. The poor child! And now it's almost Easter. Did you ever think of hiring a detective agency to look for her?'

'I did,' he sighed. 'Back on December the fifteenth. So far they've reported nothing. I thought she might have gone back to Navigation Lane. If she did, she didn't stay long enough to leave a trail. She's got to be someplace. She's only a kid, and she's never lived outside Massachusetts. If I'm lucky, she'll still be inside the Commonwealth. I may hire another agency to help out!'

The front door slammed at that moment. Mrs Corey looked up at the clock. 'Oh dear,' she sighed, 'your father's home, and supper not ready. He won't like that!' She got up stiffly, muttering under her breath at her arthritic knee, and began to bustle.

'Edith? Edith!'

'In the kitchen, dear.' He came through, having dropped his suitcoat on a chair in the living room, as usual, and clutching a small brandy glass in his hand— as usual. 'Oh, Frank. You still here? Is supper ready?'

'No, it isn't,' his wife chided him. 'It's only five o'clock. You've been asking that same question for the past thirty-five years.'

'And getting the same answer,' he chuckled. 'Something I wanted to show you, Frank. Saw it this morning at the office, and—what the devil was it?' He took a small sip of the brandy and smacked his lips. 'Best piece of work I ever did,' he said. 'When I got Tony Ricardo off on that smuggling charge, the only thing he had to pay my bill with was twenty cases of good French brandy!' He rubbed his chin, thinking. 'Of course, it was in—where did I put that newspaper!'

'In your jacket pocket,' his wife called as she checked the meatloaf in the oven.

'What's this?' he returned in exaggerated curiosity. 'New trick? I knew you were a witch when I married you, but seeing through walls is pretty hard.' He put down his glass and went out to the living-room. When he returned he was all smiles. 'Right the first time,' he crowed. 'How did you do that?'

His wife gave him an indulgent smile. 'Tricks of the trade. For the past thirty-five years you've been carrying the morning paper around in your coat pocket. Well, what is it that's so interesting?'

'I don't really know,' he laughed. 'It might only be my imagination, but the picture and the description caught my eye. It was in the first section of the *Globe* this morning—where—ah, here it is. Read that, Frank.' He passed the folded newspaper over to his son.

'I don't see how you ever get any business done,' his wife complained. 'All I ever hear about is what you read in the paper. Read it out loud, Frank.' Both men smiled affectionately at her.

'I can't tell much from the picture,' Frank said casually. 'It's a shot of a very thin girl lying on a stretcher at an accident scene, I guess. Can't tell much about the face. She's a long-haired blonde, I would guess.'

'And the story?'

'Well, the headline says, "Unknown Woman Saves Child".'

'Go on, darn it. You're worse than your father—always stopping in the middle of things.'

'Okay, okay. Let me see. "Four-year-old Robert Freeson of Hyannis owes his life today to a young as yet unidentified woman who dashed into the street to push him out of the way of a runaway truck this morning. The child received some slight cuts and bruises, and was released after treatment by Dr Hermann Thease. The woman, who was struck by the truck, is still unconscious at Cape Cod Hospital. She carried no identification. Authorities describe her as being of slight build, five feet ten inches tall, with long blonde hair. At the time of the accident she was wearing blue jeans, a bright red blouse, and a yellow plastic windbreaker. Medical authorities say that the woman is suffering from concussion and severe bruising. Anyone knowing her identity is asked to call the Hyannis Police." '

He crumpled the paper up in his hands. 'Damn!' He snapped. 'That crazy yellow windbreaker!'

'It might be?' his mother suggested. 'She's a big girl. There aren't that many big blonde girls running around the countryside.'

'True,' Frank returned, 'but slightly built? Good lord, you could never call Penny slightly built. But that damn yellow—where's Abby?'

'Across the street, playing with the Pelham girls. What yellow something?'

'It's a thin yellow windbreaker, with a broken zipper. She always wore it. It *has* to be! Get Abby for me,' he called over his shoulder as he dashed up the stairs. 'I'm going to put a few things in a bag and Abby and I are both going to Hyannis to look at this—whoever it is! Dad, would you see if you can charter a plane for us?

She woke up in the early morning hours, not understanding what had happened to her. She remembered the little boy. He had been a brilliant blob of red in his sweatsuit; she recalled the driver, blowing his horn madly and yelling something about his brakes. And she had done something. What, she could just not quite recall. And here she was lying flat on her back in some sort of narrow bed, with wires and tubes attached, and aching in every bone and muscle. She shifted her weight. It was enough to trigger the alarm in the little cubicle where a nurse kept constant watch over the Intensive Care ward. The nurse bustled in.

'Awake, are we?'

The words tickled Penny, she giggled for a second, but it hurt to move, so she quickly stopped. There's something I need to tell the nurse, she thought, but whatever it was would just not project through the maze. Funny thing, I'm tied down like an Aztec sacrifice. What did I want to ask? It came to her, but her voice cracked and failed. 'Thirsty,' she croaked. The nurse smiled and moved a drinking straw close to her lips. She sucked on it gratefully. It was taken away before she was satisfied, and she moaned an objection.

'We mustn't drink too much at one time,' the nurse proclaimed. 'A little later we'll——' Whatever it was Penny could just not stay awake long enough to find out. She slipped over the edge of sleep thinking, '*We* mustn't drink too much?' I hope I didn't use up all *her* ration too. Or was that the royal 'we'? Nurses are such important people. I don't have time to lie around here. I've got to be at work by eight o'clock!

The doctor came by for a quick check some minutes later. 'A real sleep this time, I think,' the nurse reported. 'She's uneasy. I think the bruising is starting to hurt.'

'I'll check when she wakes up,' he returned. 'Still no identification?' The Ward Secretary behind him perked up. He was eager to pin a name on his prize patient. Not only for the comfort, the publicity, but there was always that thought in the back of his mind, who pays the bills?

'No, no identification yet,' the nurse returned. 'But if it's any help she's Mrs Something or Other. She's wearing a wedding ring on her left hand. No engagement ring, but a mighty heavy gold wedding ring.'

At seven o'clock that morning, after the night shift had done its last rounds, and the sun had made a weak appearance over the town, there was an argument at the main reception desk. A man and a little girl had appeared there. The girl had a frightened expression on her face, the man looked grim and forbidding.

'I don't really care what the rules are,' he said ruthlessly. 'I mean to see this woman. And yes, the child is coming with me. We may be able to identify her. No, we don't intend to tell you anything right this minute— all we want is a quick look.'

'But she won't be awake,' the receptionist argued.

Two ambulance crewmen were in, idling close to her desk, which made her feel just a little braver than ordinarily she might.

'I don't see what that has to do with it,' Frank Corey returned. '*We* want to look at *her*; it's not necessary for her to look at us.'

'Nevertheless,' the receptionist said, 'it's against hospital policy. You'll just have to wait, I'm sorry.'

Abby was still trying to rub the sleep out of her eyes. Their late-night flight into Hyannis had led to a few—very few—hours in bed in a nearby motel, and she failed to follow all the grown-up arguments. She yanked at her father's coat sleeve and stepped in front of him. 'I wanna see my mother,' she said quietly. 'And if you don't let me, I'm gonna cry—real loud. Right here!'

The receptionist was too young to cope with this sort of blackmail. She threw in the towel. 'All right,' she said. 'She's still in ICU—the Intensive Care Unit. Mike——' She beckoned to one of the ambulance team. 'Would you lead them down to ICU? They're not to go inside, just to look. Al, maybe you'd better go along with them.' And having done her duty as she saw it, the receptionist retreated behind the novel she had been reading before they came in.

The corridor was still dark. The sun was blocked out except at either end of the hallway. The room doors were all open, and patients were stirring, but the hospital was not yet awake. Mike led them down the hall and around the corner, to where glass doors sealed off the ICU. The attending nurse, surprised to see two noses pressed against her door, came over and opened up.

'We don't allow visitors in this section,' she started out, and then stopped as Frank held up one hand.

'We're not visitors,' he said solemnly. 'We've come all the way from the Connecticut Valley to identify a patient.'

'Oh, you mean the girl who——'

'Yes, the girl who.'

'Well, don't just stand there, come in. The little girl is with you?'

'It's her mother we're looking for.'

'Dear Lord! Do come in, but quietly. No noise, young lady.'

'Yes, ma'am.'

'But the receptionist said they weren't supposed to come in,' Mike objected. 'She was very specific about that.'

The nurse was tired. Her relief had not yet appeared and, to tell the truth, she was almost continuously tired of cute little receptionists who thought they were running the hospital. 'Go back and tell her to stick her book in her ear,' she snapped. 'Come in, you two.'

Frank and Abby followed her across the semi-dark room. In the furthest corner, where only the faint light from the nursing station reflected, Penny was stretched out flat on her back, her head swathed in a massive white turban. Her left arm had slipped out from beneath the sheet and hung down slightly, fingers clenched.

'Well?' the nurse whispered.

'Mommy! That's my mother,' Abby returned softly. 'But—look, Daddy—look how skinny she is! She's—oh, Daddy!' She turned into her father's arms for comfort, and quiet tears ran down her cheek.

He was already staring at that tell-tale arm. Like a stick, it was, with none of the smooth softness he had known. Her elbow bones stuck out like great bumps. She was still wearing his wedding ring. His heart skipped a beat when he saw it. The great garish engagement ring was gone, but the simple gold band was there. He knew it had to mean something. Her arm was a mass of bruises, from wrist to the end of the short sleeve of the gown she wore. She was sleeping with her mouth slightly open, the tips of her beautiful teeth on display, her breathing heavy.

The nurse let them watch for a moment, and then she shepherded them away, back out into the enclosed nurse's station. A man hurried in, dressed in a white coat, wearing a stethoscope around his neck. 'Dr Thease,' he introduced himself. 'Well?' the nurse queried. Frank looked down at her and smiled, a lopsided sort of smile that woke the tired nurse up, despite the hour.

'Her name is Corey,' he said. 'Penelope Harris Corey.'

'Thank the Lord for that,' the doctor said. 'It's not just because she has to be *somebody*, you know, but as far as we can tell she doesn't have a penny to her name, and we've about run out of Welfare money.'

'You've got to be kidding,' he snapped. 'My God, the girl is the proud proprietor of forty million dollars!'

'You're the one who must be kidding,' the nurse returned. 'You should have seen her clothing. Threadbare. And in the middle of a real cold snap, she's outside with not much on but a little plastic wind-breaker.'

'That's right,' the doctor confirmed. 'I was on duty in the Emergency room when they brought her in. Look, there's nothing you can do here until she wakes up, and I don't know when that will be.'

'But how bad is she?' he asked. –

'More show than go,' the doctor assured him. 'Actually she's bruised from head to toe, and that's one terrible bump on the top of her head. I had to put in five or six stitches to close the wound. I'm sure she has concussion, but we won't know how bad it is until she wakes up. If you really want to know, I think her condition is due more to malnutrition rather than the accident. Corey, huh? For the record. Mrs?'

'Mrs Frank Corey,' he stated very firmly, and gave the Northampton address.

Shortly after noon they came for Penny, detached her from her miles of alarm wires, and wheeled her bed down the hall to a private room. A skilled team transferred her from the narrow ICU bed on to something more resembling a *real* bed. The room was filled with flowers. Her headache was subdued, if not gone, and her body felt—floating on air. Probably due to the injection and the paper cupful of pills, she reasoned. Everything considered, she felt not too bad. They brought her lunch, a thin soup, a piece of toast, a salad that looked as if it had lost World War II, and the tiniest bit of Jello that she could ever conceive of. One of the nursing aides stayed to help her eat.

Some little time after lunch she was the subject of attack by a very busy and very efficient LPN, who scrubbed her gently, whistled at her bruises, brushed the little tag of hair that hung outside her bandage, dabbed her gently with a little lipstick, and then stood back to admire her work. 'The little boy,' Penny asked, 'is he all right?'

'Fine. He's been released,' the nurse chuckled. 'You came off second best, didn't you. You've got visitors. Feel up to it?'

Penny felt up to anything. She felt lucky to be lying down because it seemed that her feet would be floating above the floor. It was a curious feeling. 'And if I can ever get my tongue untracked,' she mumbled, 'I've got it made. I hope I don't lose my job!' Her nose itched; she rubbed it with her left hand, and then suddenly there was another hand there to rub it for her.

'Kiss a fool?' he asked, and leaned down to caress her lips gently. It was altogether a surprise, and entirely— nice. She looked up, managing to focus her eyes on his face. His lovable face. He was smiling, and all the months of bitterness drained out of her.

'Frank?' she asked, not quite convinced by the evidence of her own two eyes.

'Frank.' He confirmed it. 'Oh Lord, Penny, what have I done to you?'

'What have *you* done to me?' she whispered huskily. 'You weren't driving the car, Frank, were you?' There was a touch of anxiety in her voice. It had all happened so suddenly she could only remember that the driver was a man—and if it had been Frank? Oh no, to run out in front of his car on purpose. What must he think of me!

'No, I wasn't driving the car,' he told her. Suddenly her breathing seemed easier. She lay back on the pillow and relaxed. 'I—I meant all this—all this mess. The last day we met in Boston, when I—I was the greatest fool in the world!'

'Yes,' she agreed. It didn't seem right to argue with him. He looked as if he wanted to hear 'yes', so she provided it.

'I don't suppose——' he stammered. 'Zimmerman?'

'I don't remember him,' she sighed. 'Was he there, too?'

'No, Penny, he was the lawyer I suggested you go to see. About the annulment. Did you?'

'Did I what, Frank? I'm not thinking very clearly today.'

'Did you go to him for an annulment?'

'Who, me?' Her surprise dug deeply into his conscience. 'No,' she managed. 'I couldn't. All I could think of was running off and hiding someplace.'

'You *couldn't* get the annulment. I don't understand, but I'm very glad you didn't. I see that you're still wearing my—our wedding ring.'

'Of course,' she said, speaking more clearly, stronger. 'I'll never take that off, Frank. I—but—Frank, I hope you're not going to be mad at me, but——'

'Me mad at *you*?' He took her hand, stroking the separate bony fingers as if they were treasures.

'Well, that's good, because I—Frank—I had to pawn the engagement ring you gave me. I ran out of money, and I couldn't find a job until a week ago. I've checked on the ring every week. If I can hold my job I can get it out of hock by the end of next month. Honestly, Frank!'

'Hey,' he said wryly, 'I wouldn't have been surprised if you had thrown it into the Bay.'

'I—I did think of that at first,' she whispered, 'but

then I knew I couldn't. It seemed like all I would ever have of you, and I had to keep it. I had to.'

He rubbed her fingers for a bit longer, then traced a line on her cheek. 'You haven't been eating much lately, have you.' It was a statement, not a question.

'I guess not,' she reflected. 'At first it was because I couldn't afford to, and then later it got to be that I couldn't stand the taste of food. In spite of all my experience, I just haven't been a good provider.'

'What the hell are you talking about?' he snapped. She tried to move away from him in the bed, but could not. Here he was, the old Frank Corey back again. Metamorphosis—in seconds. And then his face changed again. 'I promised myself I'd never do that again,' he said. 'Yell at you, I mean. Or worry about your damn money. I need you, Penny, and I don't care any more about forty million dollars. And from the look of you, you might just as well have given it away.'

'Please, Frank——' she whispered, and then gathered her strength, her courage, and her voice. 'I did,' she said in a perfectly normal tone. He stared at her.

'What?'

'I did.'

'You did what?'

'I gave all the money away. Your father helped me do it.'

'Back up,' he said through clenched teeth. 'You mean to tell me you gave the whole thing away? When?'

'In Boston, on November the fifteenth,' she said. 'After we took control of the Foundation, we voted to disband it and donated all the proceeds, money, buildings, equipment—everything, to the Dana-Farber Institute. You know, for research in children's cancer. That's why Dr Ketelman was there—to represent them.'

'Damn!' She could almost feel the bitterness that spawned wrinkles across his face. 'Why didn't you tell me then?'

'If you'll remember,' she sighed, 'you didn't give me a chance to tell you. You had everything plotted out and gave me my marching orders before I could say a word!'

'I remember,' he said. 'Have you ever been married to a bigger fool than me?'

'No,' she responded honestly, and then gasped. 'I didn't mean that you——'

'Don't apologise,' he said softly. 'I'm the one who needs to—well. I've been the biggest fool ever to come down the pike. Answer me a question, Penny?'

'If I can,' she whispered. She was getting very tired. Pleasantly tired. Frank being here made all the difference. It might truly have been the injection or the pills, but she doubted it. She was calm, peaceful, at rest, because he was where her heart was.

'Penny? Are you still awake?'

'Of course, Frank.' It was almost a lie. She was on the verge of falling away into darkness, and her eyelids were so heavy.

'Penny?' That anxious tone again. 'Why did you marry me?'

'Because I love you,' she murmured. 'I did then, and I will always. And why did you marry *me*, Frank?' She could feel herself slipping and sliding down the incline towards the dark at the bottom of the pit. She struggled against it, wanting to hear.

His answer seemed to be screened by distance, as if the words were hard come by, as if his tongue were not really prepared to handle them. 'Because I love you too, Penny,' he said. Or at least that's what she thought he said, and it was enough for the moment.

She smiled up at him, a sweet innocent loving smile. 'Take me home, Frank,' she sighed, and dropped off, sound asleep.

He sat by the bed holding her frail hand, not even daring to breathe deeply lest he wake her up. When his father and Abby tiptoed into the room an hour later he got up, flexed to restore the circulation in his arm, and went out into the hall with them.

'She looks like a scarecrow,' his father said. 'Whatever happened to her?'

'I'll tell you later,' he muttered as he scooped up his daughter and hugged her.

'Daddy, you're crying,' the child said.

'Yes, aren't I?' he returned. 'But you're not?'

'Not me,' the girl laughed. 'I'm just so glad to see Mama that I could cry! No, that's not what I meant. I won't cry. She wouldn't want me to do that. What did she say, Daddy?'

He cleared his throat. That's right, he thought, Penny wouldn't want us to cry. How little I know her! But that's soon corrected. 'Say?' he mused. 'She couldn't talk very well, love, but she asked me to take her home.'

Abby squealed with joy. The empty corridor was suddenly filled with nurses, all holding fingers to their lips. The three Coreys shushed, but the laughter hung on their lips, shone in their eyes.

'It may take some time,' Frank whispered to his father. 'Would you take Abby home today? And Dad—when she comes—she might not be able to climb stairs, and things like that.'

'I know,' his father returned. 'We'll take care of everything. You just look after yourself, so you can look after her. She looks as if she needs a great deal of looking after.'

'And you, Abby,' Frank said, 'you go along with Grandpa, and do everything you can to get things ready for your mother.'

The rest of the week passed very slowly. He spent every day and half the night at her bedside, coaxing her to eat, keeping her amused, and occasionally asking a question. She bloomed under his attention, colour returned to her cheeks, but her stubborn bones refused to retreat under smooth flesh. On Thursday they removed her head bandage.

'Nothing astonishing,' her doctor told him that afternoon. 'Funny place for a bump—right in the middle of the top of her head, no less—but the cut is healing. The stitches ought to stay in for—oh—another week. Your local doctor could take care of that. Her reactions are good. There's no further problem with the concussion. The bruises—well, none of them were terribly bad in themselves, but there are so many of them! Don't be surprised when the black and blue starts turning green. You're going to have a very colourful wife for a week or two, Mr Corey.'

'And?' he asked. 'I can hear that "and" behind everything you say.'

'And above everything, Mr Corey, see that she eats regularly! I've been giving her regular vitamin shots. Make sure she continues the regime with vitamin pills. There's no better answer for her at this stage than fresh air and a very great deal of good food. I understand that the Chairman of the Board of Selectmen will be coming by this afternoon to give her an award! If you're in a hurry, I suppose, you could take her away the day after tomorrow. With care, you understand!'

Frank told Penny about it after the doctor had left. She had slept through the entire conference. 'And lots of fresh air, and good plain food,' he finished.

'My, that sounds good.' She was well enough to laugh up at him from her slightly elevated bed. 'Hug me, Frank?'

'I would if I could find a place to hold on to,' he chuckled. 'I'm getting a little frustrated. I have this mad desire to hold you, and everything I reach is bandaged or bruised. How in the world did you get in such a shape, love?'

She knew he was talking about her bones, not her bruises. 'I don't know,' she sighed. 'I didn't do a very good job of it, did I? I never had any trouble supporting myself before *you* came along, Frank Corey, but after I left Boston I——'

'And why the devil did you leave town?' he asked. 'The next day I went along to Gainsborough Street, and there was no sign of you.'

'I couldn't help that,' she retorted, working up a little

anger to go along with the love which almost overwhelmed her. 'How could I go to Gainsborough Street when I had just given the whole house away? And there wasn't any place else to go—and—I just didn't seem to care. I went back to Navigation Lane and my lease ran out, but I just couldn't—I just didn't care, Frank. Not until I had to move, and didn't have any money.'

'And since then?'

'And—that's when I had to pawn your ring. I lived wherever I could, but for months I couldn't find a job. And then when I did, I was run down by a car. How about that for luck?'

'And it never crossed your mind to call me?'

'Every night. But—I thought—I didn't want to impose on you. I was too proud.'

'But now you don't mind?'

'Not a bit,' she laughed. 'In fact, I've something serious to ask you. When you went over to Falmouth to pick up my clothes——'

'It wasn't worth the trip,' he returned. 'Like a ragbag, it was.'

'I—well—there's something else. When you brought my clothes there was a little briefcase. The nurse put it in the cupboard. Would you bring it?' It took him but a moment. He carried the little case over to the bed and opened it for her. She fumbled around in its contents, and found the paper that she wanted.

'I've got this little problem,' she said, and took a quick look up at him. Oh what a liar you are, Penny Corey, she thought. You've got only one problem, and it's six feet tall—hardly little at all! She handed him the paper, but he was too busy studying her to notice.

'It's this bill,' she said. 'It came too late.'

'All right, I'll bite,' he chuckled. 'Too late for what?'

'It came in after we settled the forty million dollars,' she sighed. 'I—I asked my lawyer and he said——' It was too embarrassing. She just couldn't tell him.

'Come on,' he coaxed. 'I presume you're talking about my father. And what did he advise you?'

'My lawyer advised me that in Massachusetts a husband is responsible for all his wife's legal debts.'

That laughing gleam was back in his eye, and the corners of his mouth turned up. Why—he's really *not* mad at me, she thought, and how—how handsome he looks, standing there grinning at me! 'And you believed him?'

'Yes. Yes, I did,' she said defensively. 'He's your father!'

'And that's why you believed him?'

'Well, not exactly,' she sighed. 'I believed him because he added another hundred and fifty dollars to the bill for *that* advice, and I didn't dare ask him another question because I think it would have cost us a fortune—which I had just given away!'

'Us?' he queried. 'That sounds nice. And regardless of what else he might be, my father is one hell of a lawyer. Let me look at this thing.' He opened the paper and ran down the list. 'What!' he roared. At top roar, she estimated. Enough to jiggle all the audiometers in the hospital. And roaring is something I'll just have to get used to!

'Forty-two thousand, five hundred and fifty dollars for legal services! And from my own father, too. My God, does he think we have millions to give away?'

'Yes.' She clasped one of his hands and hung on. He sat down in the chair again, and waved the paper back and forth under his nose. Why, I really don't know a thing about him, but he's my husband, and I love him, she thought. And I mean to know a great deal about him in the very near future. A very great deal. 'And the bill, Frank? Can we afford to pay such a big bill?'

'Of course we can,' he laughed, 'but we won't. Let him sue us if he wants to!'

When it came time to leave the hospital she went in style. A nurse wheeled her out to the door, refusing Frank's offer to help. A limousine waited outside, chauffeured, no less. She had been walking for two days, up and down the hospital corridors, but her

husband refused to let her move a muscle. He picked
her up out of the chair with practised ease. 'Great Day,'
he whispered in her ear. 'You hardly weigh as much as
Abby does. Duck your head.' He deposited her gently
in the rear seat, then went around to enter from the
other door. He sat in the far corner as the car began to
move.

'Will you please come a little closer?' she said in an
exasperated tone.

'It's only a fifteen-minute trip,' he answered.

'So come closer, and tell him to take the long way
around,' she snapped. He grinned at her.

'Dictatorial, aren't we?' But he moved over beside
her.

'Not dictatorial at all,' she snapped. 'Frustrated.' She
squeezed closer, resting her head on his shoulder. One
of his arms went automatically around her back and
fluttered, like a bird looking for landing space.

'What's the matter?'

'I can't find a place to put my hand,' he grimaced.
'Everywhere within touching distance is off-limits.'

'Not everything,' she murmured as she curled up
against him. His right hand fell to the curve of her hip
and rested there lightly. She took his other hand in hers
and lifted it across her, to rest comfortingly on her
breast. 'There,' she sighed. 'That's never off-limits to
you, love. Now, tell him about taking the long cut.'

The air trip to the western half of the state took
slightly more than an hour, which seemed like minutes.
She leaned back against her seat and watched him,
while he watched the scenery. Another limousine met
them at the other end, and conveyed them out of town
westward, into the foothills of the Berkshires.

The house was an old wooden structure, turn-of-the-
century Victorian, with gables and bay windows
everywhere, tacked on as if they might have been an
architectural afterthought. 'We'll stay here for a time,'
he said as they sat in the car and admired. 'And then
we'll find a house for ourselves. Not too far away, I

think. All the family lives within twenty miles of here. My mother always says that she wants us close enough to visit, but far enough away so we have to make an *effort*.'

'Your mother sounds wonderful,' she said wistfully. 'I would have loved to have a mother.'

'Don't worry about it any more,' he chuckled. 'You've got one now. And a nosy one, let me tell you. She's sweetness and light with the men of the family, but she does rule the females! Up you come.'

'You don't need to do that, Frank,' she squeaked. 'I can walk. Really I can.'

'I know that, but I can't think of a better excuse for hugging, so just hush up, woman.' It seemed to be an eminently acceptable excuse, so, much against her natural inclination, she hushed. His brother George met them at the door.

'Everyone's here to welcome the bride,' he said. 'In the living room! My, you look like you've been on a ten-year diet, Penny. My mother will have you on a fattening routine within seconds.'

'Don't let him put you off the family,' Frank told her. 'He's not the only brother I've got. He's expendable.'

'Yeah, but the whole family's waiting,' George repeated. 'In the living-room.'

'No such luck,' Frank insisted. 'It's been a tiring trip, and this young lady is fresh out of the hospital. *First* she goes to bed, and then everyone can come in to be introduced.'

All nice, Penny thought, as he carried her up to the porch, but if this is a sample, when is a girl going to ever get a word in? She was giggling as her mother-in-law came to them.

'Straight down the hall,' Mrs Corey said. 'We've converted Grandfather's old study for you both—on the second floor.'

'I feel like an overgrown Barbie doll,' she told him as he carried her down the hall and into a large quiet room. It contained bedroom furniture, but bookcases still lined the walls. The bed was huge; an Emperor size, so to speak, with heavy wooden headboards and footboards. Light streamed in from three large windows, and she caught just a small glimpse of a garden outside, at the back of the house.

'Hush, woman,' he whispered in her ear. 'You're being honoured. That's Great-grandfather's bed. Brought it with him when he came over from the old country. You don't find that sort of hand-carving these days.'

'I—I know I'm impressed,' she whispered back, 'but what a terrible expense it must have been to bring this all the way from Ireland.'

'From Ireland?' he bellowed. 'Say, have you got it wrong, lady. The family name was originally Corelli, but when Great-grandfather went through Ellis Island it got shortened to Corey. Ireland, indeed! And that to the finest family in Genoa.'

'Good lord,' she giggled, 'you mean I'm Italian now?'

'Better believe it, lady! Wait until you see the Columbus Day celebration!'

'And the bathroom is through here,' Mrs Corey told them, throwing open the other door in the room. 'Isn't that nice? It used to be the storage room for the kitchen. Didn't they do a nice job, Frank?'

'They certainly did,' he agreed, 'but I've got to get this girl to bed.'

'For medicinal reasons only, I suppose,' his mother said with a perfectly straight fact. 'I brought her a couple of nightgowns and a bedjacket. In the wardrobe, there. I thought that would be enough for a few days. We'll go down to town some day soon and get her something more. Now, don't be long. All the others are waiting. I suppose you don't need any help undressing your wife?' Again that perfectly solemn face, but as her mother-in-law faced the light, Penny could see the beginning of a wickedly teasing gleam in her eyes.

'For God's sake, Mother!' he exclaimed. His mother

giggled and left them alone. 'Now then,' he said as he sat her down on the bed. 'We get you all noodled up, and we'll run the relatives by for you. It'll take a week before you remember all the names. All right?'

'Frank? I forgot something.'

'What?' He was unbuttoning her blouse, and the touch of his warm fingers on her bare skin was doing more than giving her a chill. It also disturbed all her thought processes. She struggled to get her mind back on track. 'Your ring,' she said. 'I forgot your ring.'

'Good,' he returned. Her blouse was off, and he was working on her shoes at the moment. 'Forget the ring. I took care of it. You never did like it anyway, did you?'

'Honest Injun?'

'Honest Injun.'

'I—no, I never liked it. It seemed more like a brand of possession than the seal to a promise.'

He looked at her tenderly. 'I suppose that's why I got it,' he sighed.

And look at me, she yelled at herself. Little Miss Independence. I'll never depend on a man for anything. Not me! So why am I standing here like a fool, shivering, while he takes off my tights. Lord, Penny—Corey, you have turned into the biggest patsy in the world. He's—Lord—and I love it!

'Well, that seems to take care of—oh, how could I have forgotten!' His hands reached for the single front snap that held her bra in position. It fell away, leaving her breasts to sway into his hands. 'My poor little lady,' he said softly as his hands gently caressed her. 'I feel so damn guilty, love, when I look at how bruised and battered you are.' His head had bent to kiss where his hands had been wandering. She put both her hands on his cheeks and brought his head up again.

'Don't, Frank,' she appealed to him. 'Don't be guilty, don't be sad. It's all behind us. We both share the guilt, and now I want to share the happiness with you. I want you to think of me as—as sexy green!' She pushed his head down to where it was.

'Ah,' he chuckled. 'Then you don't mean "don't" to this?' His words were muffled in the softness of her.

'Yes,' she sighed. 'I mean—I—I don't know what I mean. I never should have married a lawyer. Don't stop!'

'Frank! Penny! Hurry up, for goodness' sakes!' It was his mother, just on the other side of the door. He shook his head in disgust, and stepped back from her. 'Family!' he snorted.

There was a wisp of silk hanging in the wardrobe. It hardly seemed to merit more description. She managed to raise her arms while he dropped it over her head. It fell down across her body, from neck to ankles, and hid not a thing. 'Your mother bought me this,' she gasped.

'There *has* to be something else to go with this thing,' he muttered. 'How about this?' It was a padded bedjacket, with a Chinese dragon poised across its front. She offered her arms again, and he slid it clumsily around her. 'Well, that's half the show gone,' he chuckled. 'Now, into bed with you. And don't wiggle a muscle. Some of my brothers are not to be trusted.'

'I'll bet *they* say the same about *you*,' she said as she made her way under the covers. He helped as she settled against the pile of pillows that elevated her, and then dropped a kiss on her forehead. 'Who first?' he asked.

'Abby,' she stated firmly. 'I want to see my daughter.' He opened the door, and the deluge followed.

CHAPTER ELEVEN

PENNY managed to straggle out of the bedroom at eight o'clock, leaving him peacefully asleep behind her. She carefully rearranged the covers, ran her fingers through his hair, and closed the door behind her. A kiss would have been wonderful, but impossible. The robe her mother-in-law loaned her could have gone twice around her midriff, but hardly reached an inch above her knees. She had locked it on securely with a large belt. But there was nothing she could do with her head. It buzzed and ached and pained—no little part because of his grunted, 'Well, I hope you're satisfied now!'

That had been at one in the morning when he stumbled out of the warm bed and tried to find an ice-pack for her. He had tramped down the hall with all the grace of the lead elephant in a herd, threatening destruction to half the house until his mother came to his rescue.

And now she was bedraggled, tired, confused, but unwilling to lie abed. She pushed open the door into the big warm kitchen and was amazed to find it crowded. It seemed as if all the women of the family were there, in various forms of undress, around a loaded breakfast table. The conversation stopped as soon as she appeared.

'Wow!' Marion exclaimed. Harry's wife? She just couldn't remember. Everyone else was dead quiet. And why not? Who else in the house had an ice-bag strapped to the top of her head with a long but slipping elastic bandage? Who else was dressed in a see-through nightgown chosen by her mother-in-law? And the robe that tried to hide it all was doing a damnably poor job.

Judith scooted her chair over to make room at the table. Bill's wife? Penny managed to make it to the table, and almost collapsed into a chair. 'If you want to sue, I know a lawyer,' Judith laughed.

'Man!' Marion shook her head slowly. 'I always knew Frank was a peculiar fellow, but never a wife-beater!'

'Marion!' Mrs Corey cautioned.

'Well, look at the poor child! What happened, Penny?'

Penny was too embarrassed to raise her eyes from the plate. 'I . . . I . . .' she stammered. 'I was—I bumped my noggin on the headboard of the bed.'

'Right on top of the bump you already had? Poor kid!' The room filled with commiseration. Nobody, thank God, asked how it happened. Perhaps that was what Ethel had been on to when her mother 'shushed' her. Penny looked down at the flower patterns on her plate, wishing her head would fall off instead of just aching. How good it had been until that crazy moment!

When Frank came in she had shed her bedjacket, thrown off her sheet, and stretched out like a huge cat, waiting. He had gone into the bathroom and come back, wet-haired, wearing a robe. She could hardly hold still. Women were not supposed to be so eager, she told herself, but could not believe it. She ached for him, and he stood there and looked. Just looked.

'Is that all you plan for tonight?' she asked sarcastically.

'Hey, it's some sight,' he chuckled. 'And you did say we should be happy about it. You're all—all you, black and green and yellow——'

'Frank Corey,' she snarled, 'I've waited months for this. I've read about it, seen it in all the films, and you're just going to stand there and ogle me! I've got a terrible itch I can't scratch!'

'But don't forget, the doctor said no excitement!'

'Damn the doctor!'

'That's no way to talk,' he said mournfully. 'He's one hell of a good doctor. You should see his bill!'

'Do we measure doctors now by the method we use

for lawyers? According to how high their bills are? Dammit, Frank, I—I know it's not modest, and all that—that stuff, but I can't wait.'

'Ah, but one of us has to be careful, and I guess it's me.'

'Are you teasing me, Frank Corey? If you are I'll kill you. I swear to God I'll—well, if you must be careful, come and be careful beside me.' She patted the bed. He slipped out of his robe, totally natural, totally naked. She gasped. It was the first time she had ever seen a male wholly naked. And he wanted her; there was no way he could hide it. 'Hurry up,' she pleaded.

'I can't hurry,' he laughed, 'that's not how it's done, girl, especially with somebody who's a bag of bones! Slow and easy is the motto!'

'So that's what it is,' she snapped. 'You don't dare. You don't have the guts! You think you'll get splinters!' And that had done it. The tingle where the tip of his tongue touched base on each of her breasts as he shoved the straps of her gown aside. The warmth pursued her as his hands slipped up and down from hip to warm pulsing breast, ghosting like the touch of an errant wind—but trailed seconds later by an explosion of excitement that she had never known before. The heat of contact as he kissed her, while she ran her hands up and down his iron frame, wishing she knew more about how to turn a man on. And then, full of laughter and wild excitement, his hand had slipped down, down, over the small roundness of her stomach and had stopped to touch that one magic place, that one point of contact she had never even thought about before. The touch had been so exquisite, so exciting, that she had squealed in pleasure and bounced up in the bed—to bang her head, of course, right on the bump—against the ornately carved oak headboard. And that had been the end of her night!

'And I hope you're satisfied,' Frank had grouched as he stumbled off to effect emergency repairs.

And then a little later, 'Where are you going?' she called after him. 'We could——'

'With a half-pound ice-bag on your skull?' he grumbled. 'I need a shower. A nice long cold shower!'

And how could you tell a group of sisters-in-law, and his mother, something like that? Or for that matter, how could she tell Frank? Because she had been very unsatisfied. Very unsatisfied indeed!

'I never used to be so clumsy,' she sighed. 'What's the breakfast drill?'

'As you see,' her mother-in-law said. The table was loaded with platters of scrambled eggs, toast, and sausages. 'I do for all the women, but I expect each one of you to take care of your own man.'

To her amazement Penny found herself hungry. She ladled a full plate, supplemented by a mug of coffee and set to. The conversation washed over her head, until suddenly she looked up from her plate and found everyone looking at her. Embarrassed, she looked herself over. 'Am I losing my ice-pack?' she asked.

'No, love,' sister Ethel said. 'My mother—our mother—has just made one of her regular pithy comments. The rest of us are accustomed to it.'

'I—I'm sorry,' Penny apologised. 'I think I was woolgathering. What did you say, Mrs—er—Mother?'

'I said,' her mother-in-law repeated very firmly, 'that all this trouble that you and Frank are having is all due to one thing. God is angry with you.'

'God?' Penny was stunned. She had occasionally gone to church, but not as a regular thing. 'Why would he bother with someone as unimportant as me?'

'He marks the sparrow's fall,' her mother-in-law stated flatly.

'Good Lord, I didn't know that!' Penny had heard the quotation somewhere or another, but missed the connection. Her headache added to the confusion. Why me? Are they all missing a few marbles? She said it aloud. 'Why me?'

'Because you haven't been married properly,' Mrs

Corey said. 'A girl ought to be married in church, with a long white dress, and music, and all the family. That's the way it's done. Going off to hide in the office of some judge is not the way to do it. You'd both better get married if you expect anything to go right for you. Ah, Frank. It's about time you showed up. Look what you've done to this poor girl. You should be ashamed of yourself.'

'I am,' Frank said. He was leaning on the door jamb, looking every bit as desolate as Penny, but without a matching ice-bag. There was a bustle at the table as the other women fled. He came over and thumped himself down beside his wife. 'And it will all go away as soon as Penny and I are church-married?'

'The very day,' his mother assured him. 'Well?'

'Penny.' He turned to concentrate on her. 'I forgot something last night. When I said you needn't worry about that engagement ring, I meant that I had already taken care of it. I reclaimed it—and then sold the thing off. Now, if I may have your hand without you hitting me with it?' He picked up her left hand from off the table. She held her breath while he reached into the pocket of his robe and pulled out a lovely sapphire ring, the blue central jewel circled by tiny diamond chips. It fitted perfectly. 'Like that one better?' he asked. She had no answer. No words, that is. Moving her head very carefully, she kissed him gently.

'Now,' he continued, smiling, 'what do you say we try to get rid of this jinx? Let's get married again.'

St Edward's Church was loaded to breaking with flowers on that warm morning. Spring was almost at hand, and the windows were open. The sweet fragrance of hyacinth filled the air, and a slight breeze brought inside the clarity of valley air. Ethel served as her only bridesmaid, Abby was flower girl, and her father-in-law gave Penny away. The church was packed with friends and relatives, and small children's voices could be heard from time to time during the service. She screwed up her nerves when the organ sounded, poised at the far end of the long bright aisle where Frank waited. And she remembered absolutely nothing of all the rest of the beautiful Episcopal service. Nothing.

The reception, she was given to understand much later, lasted for six hours after the wedding couple raced off. They went exactly ten miles, to the Hotel Jeffrey, in Amherst. 'What an elegant place,' she murmured in his ear. Somehow or another he was carrying her in his arms again. 'We must see the lounge,' she added. 'Marion says it's beautiful.'

'Yeah,' he said, and headed straight for the lifts. A bellman appeared at his side, flashing a key and a big smile, another trotted behind them with a single bag.

'Frank,' she said as the lift door closed on them, 'he's only got *your* bag. I won't have any clothes to wear. Didn't you stop by my room and pick up my bag? What will I wear?'

'Ain't it wonderful,' he returned. 'Wonderful!'

'But Frank, what will all the other guests say?'

'Not a word, Penny Corey. I've got a key. The door will be locked behind us, and all the other guests can go down and admire the lounge, for all I care. Lord, lady, I believe you're putting on weight!' He put her down just outside their door and waited while the bellman unlocked the door and stood aside. There was some interchange between the three of them, and the two hotel employees left—with very large smiles on their faces.

She wandered into the room. 'Hey,' he yelled at her. 'Everything by the book, lady, or we'll never break the jinx!' He pulled her back out into the corridor, picked her up again, and marched smartly inside, closing the door behind them with a click of his heel. When he set her down this time he was breathing hard. 'You really are putting on weight,' he stated. She looked around, admiring. The decorations were in gold and bronze, salted and peppered by only a slight amount of furniture, but featuring one very large bed. Penny went

over to it, grabbed all the pillows, and set them up as a
barrier between the body of the bed and its massive
headboard.

Before she could turn round he came up behind her.
She felt the zipper slide down her back, and her dress
was gone. In a matter of seconds they were on the bed,
desperately entangled with each other.

'Good Lord,' he muttered into her neck. 'I didn't
think this day would ever come! I've never been so
frustrated in all my life! Never!' And all the while his
hands were busy, roaming up and down her soft clear
skin, taking little samples of her thighs, her breasts, her
ears, her mouth, while he shed his own clothes.

'Frustrated,' she managed to squeeze out above the
wild sensations of her body. 'You don't know what
frustration is. I'll show you frustration!'

This time, when his fingers arrived back at that very
special spot, she was not really *ready*—who the devil
could ever be *ready* for such a feeling—but when she
involuntarily jumped, her head was cushioned by all those
pillows, and she wiggled her way back down to him before
he noticed. Her pulse was racing, her feet tingled, and
everything in between was on fire. 'I don't know what to
do, Frank,' she whispered in his ear. 'Show me!' He did.

Three hours later she moved gently away from him.
He was fast asleep. The first time had been an
adventure; the second time had blown her mind! He
deserved some rest, she told herself resolutely. Her
breasts were tender to her touch, and her hips felt as if
they had been under a pile-driver. But she was willing
to suffer some more, if he insisted. Unfortunately, she
couldn't wake him up.

She lay on her side and watched him. His mouth was
slightly open, perspiration beaded his forehead, and he
had the biggest, most satisfactory grin on his face. She
leaned over him and wiped his forehead dry with her
long hair. He looked so handsome, she told herself,
almost beautiful. It took a lot of digging, but I finally
uncovered my hidden treasure!

And now, Penny Corey, she demanded of herself, are *you* satisfied? Are you happy? She knew the answer to the second question. Happy, yes. More so than ever in her life before. More so than anybody in this hotel, more so than—one of Frank's eyes were blinking at her. She rolled over on top of him and shook him by the shoulders.

'Frank Corey, you big faker,' she yelled. 'You double-crossing low-life. Asleep! Hah!' And there was the answer to her first question. No, I'm not satisfied. Not yet. But how do you lead this male animal to water and make him drink? She rolled back off him, lay flat on her back, and folded her arms under her head. His eyes shifted from her face downward, and she felt a little tingle of excitement. That's one of his interests, she told herself—or I should have said two!

'Frank,' she said softly, 'now I really don't have any clothes to wear. You tore my briefs to pieces, and broke the zipper on my dress. We might have to hang around for two or three days before I get some more clothes.'

'Terrible,' he groaned, 'but given enough incentive, I might be able to find something for us to do.'

'And in the meantime I'll have to stay in bed,' she said very primly.

'Yes. What a terrible mess.' He was having trouble keeping a straight face. He reached over and stroked her tender breasts. 'Did *you* have something in mind?'

'Well—yes, I do,' she said bravely. 'I'm broke, Frank, and I need some money badly.'

'Maybe you shouldn't have given everything away,' he chuckled. His hand slipped down to her groin.

'Stop that,' she snapped. 'I'm trying to think. How can I think when you do that!' Much to her surprise he stopped. For about ten seconds she wished he wouldn't be so darn obedient, and then she recovered her train of thought.

'Your mother had us all in the kitchen yesterday,' she continued. 'She's offering a cash prize—five hundred dollars—for the appearance of her first grandson. I *do* need the money. Do you suppose we could enter the contest?'

'Mercenary. I knew it!' But he was laughing at her. His money devil seemed to have disappeared. 'Five hundred dollars, no strings attached?'

'I don't know about strings,' she murmured. His hand was wandering again, destroying her ability to concentrate. 'Your mother is a better manipulator than your father, and he's some sort of shark!'

'It might be a very hard prize to win, with lots of competition,' he chuckled. 'Roll over here, and let's talk about it.'

'Talk won't win any prizes,' she giggled, but she rolled over towards him anyway.

Harlequin Presents

Coming Next Month

959   THE CALL OF HOME Melinda Cross
After her father's death and her mother's recovery from her breakdown,
an American painter returns to her childhood haunt to heal her own
wounds—and comes up against a man who's as much in need of love as
she is.

960   WOMAN OF HONOUR Emma Darcy
Labeled a home-wrecker when a certain lawyer's brother-in-law neglected
to mention his marriage, an Australian chef turns workaholic. But guess
who her next Dial-A-Dinner Party client is?

961   TRY TO REMEMBER Vanessa James
A distraught amnesiac and a forceful merchant banker search from
Devon to Morroco for something to jolt her memory. But what really
knocks her for a loop is her feelings for him.

962   A MAN POSSESSED Penny Jordan
Fate brings an old friend of a widow's late husband back into her life, the
man who'd rejected her in the midst of her bleak marriage. But it seems
he'd desired her, after all.

963   PASSIONATE VENGEANCE Margaret Mayo
A London designer finds herself fired on trumped-up charges. Her
reputation's smeared. So the job at Warrender's Shoes seems like a
lifeline—until she discovers her boss's motives in hiring her.

964   BACHELOR IN PARADISE Elizabeth Oldfield
The soap opera star a British author interviews in Florida isn't the vain
celebrity she'd expected. He lives frugally, disappears every Wednesday,
declares parts of his life "off-limits"—and fascinates her to no end!

965   THE ARRANGEMENT Betsy Page
Marry the woman from Maine or forfeit control of the family business,
an uppercrust Bostonian warns his son. But the prospective bride is as
appalled by the arrangement as the groom—so they have one thing in
common, at least.

966   LOVE IN THE MOONLIGHT Lilian Peake
A young journalist wants to warn her sister in Cornwall that the man
she's dallying with is a heartbreaker. But how can she—when she's still in
love with the man herself?

Available in March wherever paperback books are sold, or through
Harlequin Reader Service:

In the U.S.
P.O. Box 1397
Buffalo, N.Y.
14240-1397

In Canada
P.O. Box 603
Fort Erie, Ontario
L2A 5X3

Six exciting series for you every month... from Harlequin

Harlequin Romance·
The series that started it all

Tender, captivating and heartwarming...
love stories that sweep you off to faraway places
and delight you with the magic of love.

◆

Harlequin Presents·
Powerful contemporary love stories...as individual as the women who read them

The No. 1 romance series...
exciting love stories for you, the woman of today...
a rare blend of passion and dramatic realism.

◆

Harlequin Superromance®
It's more than romance... it's Harlequin Superromance

A sophisticated, contemporary romance-fiction
series, providing you with a longer,
more involving read...a richer mix of complex plots,
realism and adventure.

Harlequin
American Romance™
Harlequin celebrates the American woman...

...by offering you romance stories written about American women, by American women for American women. This series offers you contemporary romances uniquely North American in flavor and appeal.

◆

Harlequin Temptation™
Passionate stories for today's woman

An exciting series of sensual, mature stories of love...dilemmas, choices, resolutions... all contemporary issues dealt with in a true-to-life fashion by some of your favorite authors.

◆

Harlequin Intrigue
Because romance can be quite an adventure

Harlequin Intrigue, an innovative series that blends the romance you expect... with the unexpected. Each story has an added element of intrigue that provides a new twist to the Harlequin tradition of romance excellence.

Harlequin Books·

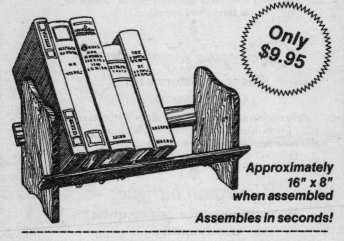